Copyright © 2020 Mishana Khot

Mishana Khot

Welcome to the Zoo

All rights reserved, including the right of reproduction in whole or in part in any form.

Published by: Independently published

Website: www.mishanakhot.com

Cover Design by: Rujuta Mistry

Book Layout by: Ravinder Nain

Welcome to the Zoo

Mishana Khot

For my father
who taught us
how to be brave and fight our own battles,
how to jump fearlessly and run fast,
how to put up a tent on a windy day,
how to grout the bathroom tiles,
how to tell a shaggy dog story,
how to be kind to animals,
how to ride our bicycles at full speed,
how to build a bonfire,
and other essential life skills

But above all,
how to believe in magic.

Table of Contents

Introduction
Character List
Puppy Snuffles and the Devil's Own Hounds
The Honorary Khots
An Egyptian Mummy in Fort
Catching Crabs for Dinner
Meet Mr. Waffles
Fairies in the Tree House
Sundays are for Dynamite Fishing
Nobody Likes the New Governess
Whirlpool Weekend
Izzy's All-You-Can-Eat Guppy Buffet
Finger-Flavoured Ice-Cream
Belly Flops and Nose Dives
Black Magic Frankie
Fireworks in the Fort
The Great Christmas Horror Show
The Egyptian Mummy Returns
Hairy Tales
Kannada Sir
Ghost Stories
The Terrible Injection Story
Fireflies in Jars
A Note from the Author
Acknowledgements

Introduction

High up in the misty Western Ghats, nestled amidst lush tropical forests and swaying fields of sugarcane, there is a little town called Belgaum. Time flows like golden honey here, slow and sweet. People drop by for a cup of tea and a comfortable chat with their neighbours. Children dawdle on their way to school. When the sun sinks in a glory of orange, buffaloes amble down the main road, forcing traffic to wait as they head to their barns for the night.

These are the early 90s and the frenetic dash of the rat race has not yet arrived in Belgaum. Our days are filled with grace and harmony and the world is as it should be.

At the city centre, the teeming markets are a medley of sound and colour. Bakeries and sweetmeat shops don't bother with signboards; they know that the yeasty fragrance of freshly baked bread or the sweet cardamom-laced aroma of *gulab jamuns* will beckon to customers. Farmers from nearby villages rattle up in rickshaws to sell fruit and vegetables that glisten with the morning dew, and animated haggling wars take place between shoppers and sellers.

On the outskirts of the city, away from the crowded streets, there is an ancient fort, complete with ramparts and a moat. Once upon a time, the fierce cavalries and glittering royal retinues of the Mughals and the Marathas paraded through the Fort. When the British arrived, they fell in love with the sun-dappled environs and built sprawling bungalows with pretty gardens for themselves.

Over 800 years later, the Fort still stands strong. But now, instead of kings and conquerors, it is the playground of the four hyper-imaginative kids who live in one of the bungalows here. Tangle-haired and sun-browned, accompanied by friends just as wild as they are, tripping over smiling dogs that careen along beside them, and surrounded by their many cats, guinea pigs, rabbits, peacocks, and turtles, they've formed a retinue of their own.

Welcome to the zoo.

Character List

AJI

Aji is 72 years old. She's tall and graceful, ties her silver hair up into a bun and has soft wrinkly hands with long fingers. She always smells of Ponds powder and Lux soap, and she wears saris with flowers on them. Aji picks up our cats many times in the day to pet them but she always strokes them backwards. We know that cats hate having their fur ruffled, but our cats seem to love it. Aji says she loves all of us equally, but we know that Kuku, the *baabloo* of our family, is her not-so-secret favourite.

DADDY

Daddy is 44 years old. He whizzes around the house and the garden engrossed in projects of his own, and can build treehouses and solar cookers with his bare hands. When we were very little, he built a big motorcycle with a shiny blue tank. Every evening, Mummy and he piled all four of us onto it and we thundered off to visit friends around Belgaum. After Mummy passed away last year, Daddy put away the motorbike and bought an old Fiat to drive us more sedately around town.

MAHI

That's me! I'm 11 years old. I like to read my books or write stories, and sometimes I lock myself in the bathroom just to get some quiet time to read. Because I'm the big sister, it's my job to make sure the other three don't do anything stupid like drowning in the well or falling off the roof. I love the cats and the rabbits most and am very good at picking ticks out of their fur or maggots out of their ears.

IZZY

Izzy is 9 years old, but he's short for his age. He's waiting for the growth spurt that everyone assures him is coming, but he's as strong and sturdy as a small tractor and if he punches one of us in the stomach (which he often does), it takes a while to catch our breath. He climbs trees faster than anyone we know, can hold his open palm over a flame, and can steal chocolate bars from the cupboard without rustling the wrappers.

RITU

Ritu is 7 years old, with skinny arms and legs. She twirls her hair in in her sleep so when she wakes up, there are big tangled knots all around her head. She looks meek but if we bully her, she scratches us with her small sharp nails, drawing blood and leaving scars that last for months. She always has a cat weaving around her ankles or sleeping under her sweater.

KUKU

Kuku is 6 years old and with her big eyes and chubby cheeks, looks like butter wouldn't melt in her mouth. She likes to eat wedges of Amul butter and is terrified of being put inside the lovebird enclosure when it's her turn to clean it. She's the pet of the family and gets away with anything just because she's cute, but sometimes we smack her just to keep her in her place.

RUM AND RAISIN

We've always had dogs in our bungalow but they're not allowed into the house. We rescued Rum and Raisin when they were stray pups on the side of the road, and they now have the run of the garden. They think they're the official bodyguards for the four of us and bark outside our window all night to let us know they're keeping watch. They wait patiently outside the door for us to wake up in the morning and then they spend the rest of the day begging for snacks, gnawing the itchy-scratchy fleas that bite them, and tripping us up when we're in the garden.

ECLIPSE

Eclipse was the only black kitten in a litter of pretty tortoiseshell kittens at a friend's place. Because human beings are stupid, they think black cats are unlucky, so he was the only one that nobody wanted. The first time we met him, we fell in love with his coal-black spiky fur and shiny green eyes. When the owner said they would have to drown him because that's what happened to unwanted kittens, Daddy plopped him into our laps and we took him home, and he's been our baby ever since.

MR. WAFFLES

We grew up on Brer Rabbit stories so it was only a matter of time before we began begging Daddy to get us a rabbit. When we brought Mr. Waffles home, we discovered a shocking secret about him, but you'll find that out later in the book.

We also have a few guinea pigs who nibble our fingers, a pea hen that somehow survives being chased by Rum and Raisin, a big ugly turtle named Anaconda that only Izzy loves, and an assortment of rainbow coloured lovebirds who don't do much except chirp and look at us with beady eyes.

CHAPTER ONE

Puppy Snuffles and the Devil's Own Hounds

Even though it was only five in the evening, the sky was already grey and overcast outside. The four of us were sitting around Aji, drinking our milky tea and telling her what we had done at school that day.

"And then he flung the chalk at us, Aji! For no reason!" Izzy was breathless with indignation as he told us about his teacher, who apparently hated Izzy and every other boy in his class. "And I wasn't even talking…."

"But you must have been doing something," said Ritu sensibly. "Why else would he throw the chalk at you?" She was perched on a stool, balancing a mug of tea with Eclipse, our lazy black cat, fast asleep her lap.

We like to joke that when Ritu is around, Eclipse's feet don't touch the ground all day. The minute she gets home from school, she lifts him up onto her shoulder and keeps him there till she goes to bed. He sits on her chair at the dining table, rubber-necking around her elbow to grab a morsel. He dozes on her lap at study time. He waits patiently outside her bathroom at bath time. Nobody knows what he does during the day when Ritu is at school.

"No! I'm telling you I didn't do anything. I was sitting there quietly, just drawing, and he just started yelling…"

"You were drawing? In your Maths class?" Kuku dipped her glucose biscuit carefully into her mug. She was trying to get it just soggy enough to melt in her mouth, but not so soggy that it collapsed in a yucky mess into her tea. "That's why he threw the chalk at you."

"I… but I …I didn't…" Izzy had nothing to say in his defence, so he reached over and knocked Kuku's biscuit into her tea. She shrieked and kicked him in the shin. At 6 years old, she may have been the runt of the litter, but she was already stronger than Ritu, who was a year older.

Izzy leapt up in glee to retaliate. He spent his television time re-watching *Rambo* and *Rocky* and was always primed to fight. Although he was only three feet tall, he had been practising his dropkicks on Kuku, and had recently started drawing a six-pack on his rotund belly with a marker pen.

Aji put her arm out to hold him off and protect her *baabloo*. "No, Izzy, don't you try that. She's your baby sister; you can't beat her like this."

Aji's favourite chair is placed next to the phone, and she sits here all day, exactly at the centre of our home and our lives. This is our favourite part of the day – coming home after school to tell her what we did and who got into trouble today.

"But she started…."

"That's enough from you. You're 9 years old – you're supposed to be older and wiser. Behave yourself now or I'll tell Daddy when he comes home."

Izzy snarled at Kuku and sat down again, muttering darkly to himself.

Aji looked outside and turned to us. "Come on now, all of you take your cycles and go out for a ride. Go burn off some energy before it starts raining. You've only got about an hour and then you'll be stuck indoors for the rest of the evening."

As the eldest at the ripe old age of 11 years, it was my job to round up the team, especially the smallies. Izzy and I were the biggies, and we knew that the lowly smallies required our supervision at all times.

I tipped my cup to drain my tea and began to shove the others off their seats. Ritu slid Eclipse off her lap and onto the chair so gently that it didn't even open its eyes, and we hurried to pull on our shoes and raincoats.

Out on the road, the air crackled with electricity and the wind buffeted us as we pedalled. We responded to the primal thrill in the atmosphere, hooting and leaning forward into the wind, trying to beat the dark clouds that were rolling in behind us.

We lived quite some distance from the city, so there was rarely any traffic inside the Fort. The roads were quiet and deserted and perfect for our cycle rides. But the solitude also meant that if someone wanted to do something secret, they came into the Fort to do it. We often spotted couples locked in fervent embraces on the ramparts, or stumbled upon people huddled over handmade cigarettes in the back roads.

But none of these people were ever of any interest to us. The ones whom we stopped to observe were those who came in with big gunny sacks or cane baskets tied to the backs of their bikes. They'd park in a secluded spot and surreptitiously unload their cargo, cutting open the strings before jumping onto their bikes and zooming off.

It was quite common for people to abandon unwanted puppies or kittens inside the Fort, but we were always happy to take them straight home to make them ours.

So when Ritu spotted the moving grass by the side of the road and screeched, we skidded to a halt. Throwing our cycles onto the ground, we plunged into the waist-high reeds to investigate.

Sure enough, someone had left eight puppies in a sack in the middle of the overgrown field. They were wriggling and squealing, and we fell upon them with cries of delight. We picked them up in each hand, covering them with kisses, and then shushed each other. Our favourite part about puppies was holding them up to listen to the hot breath snuffling in our ears.

As we stood there letting them lick our faces and whisper in our ears, an uncle from a neighbouring bungalow hurried by. He stopped to scream at us to get out of the grass before we were bitten by snakes and then rushed off, eager to get home to his cup of tea.

"We'd better go," said Ritu. A crack of thunder made her look up at the skies. "But we can't leave them here."

"We have to take them home," Izzy puffed, already tucking his t-shirt into his shorts, and stuffing a puppy into the neck of his t-shirt. "This field floods when it rains, and they won't be able to climb out." The puppy wriggled at his belly and he patted it before putting another one inside and adjusting them on either side of his ribs.

None of us questioned this decision. The puppies were rolling about at our feet and nibbling our ankles and we were already in love. The smallies helped to slide a puppy into each of the giant pockets on my raincoat. Kuku and Ritu had matching wire baskets on the handlebars of their cycles, so we loaded the rest of the puppies into the baskets.

We cycled carefully home, just as a big angry cloud burst overhead. Lightning sliced across the sky and the rain began to come down in sheets. It poured down the backs of our necks and blew our hoods off our heads, but we cycled in a steady line, adjusting the puppies now and then.

As we wheeled our cycles into the shed in our bungalow, we found Kanappa pulling on his waterproof pants, ready to set off in search of us. Kanappa had once been valet and butler to my grandfather, back when Daddy was a teenager. But now that our grandfather was no more, Kanappa was head gardener and housekeeper, as well as lunchbox dropper-off for us. His wife, Tulsi Bai was our cook and our favourite shoulder to cry on, second only to Aji.

Our bungalow had an outhouse - a long block of small independent rooms in the backyard, a relic from colonial times when every household had staff quarters nearby. Now, like many bungalows in Belgaum, the rooms were occupied by tenants. Kanappa lived with Tulsi Bai in the biggest room in the outhouse and we often "visited them" to present our drawings or drink milky tea with them before school.

Kanappa was Daddy's partner in crime and was always up for a new project. They were often found smoking the vile *beedis* that Kanappa loved and arguing about how to build a solar cooker or when to reinforce the compound fences. He pretended to be deaf when he didn't want to do something, but if we were trying to sneak around the garden for one of our pranks, he'd hear our softest footsteps and come rushing out to catch us.

Tulsi Bai and Kanappa had rocked us to sleep as babies, burped us when we cried, and watched us setting off on our first day of school. They spent a considerable amount of time pulling us off each other during our wrestling matches or preventing us from falling out of trees.

When he saw us cycling in, Kanappa breathed a sigh of relief and hurried us indoors. We entered the house, dripping water onto the floor and shivering violently, and Tulsi Bai gasped and began to scold as she peeled the wet clothes off us.

But then the puppies started appearing.

One by one, Tulsi Bai pulled puppies out of our pockets and from our shirts, her eyes growing wider with each puppy. We were put straight into the bathroom to be scrubbed down, in case we had picked up fleas from the puppies. Faced with raucous arguments that the puppies would have to be bathed too, she threw her hands up and let us take them in for a bath. We scrubbed the puppies while Tulsi Bai scrubbed us.

Half an hour later, the four of us and eight puppies emerged from the bathroom, fragrant with Mediker lice shampoo and Lifebuoy.

Although she scolded us for using our own towels to wrap and dry 'those mongrels', Aji was too soft-hearted to leave the tiny puppies out in the middle of a storm. So while the thunder rumbled all night and rain poured down on our tiled roof and gushed into the gutters, we spent a cosy evening feeding the pups warm milk and bread, and eating warm milk and bread ourselves.

When it was time to go to sleep, we made a bed of soft cardboard boxes and old bedsheets in the bathroom, and tucked the puppies in for a comfortable night.

As we whispered to each other in bed that night, we knew we'd have to put up a big fight the next day. Daddy was out for the evening and didn't know we were harbouring a whole batch of puppies in our bathroom, but he would find out as soon as he got home. We knew that we wouldn't be able to keep all eight of them, but we thought we could manage about six.

"Just turn on the waterworks, all of you," Izzy advised wisely. It took a cold heart to refuse us, especially when faced with the trembling chins of Kuku and Ritu. This was going to be a tough case to plead, but sometimes it worked. If it didn't, the puppies were dropped off at the Fish Market, where they grew into greedy fatties who slept in the sunshine all day and dined on fish at night.

If the dog population at home was thin that month, we were often allowed to keep one or two of the strays we brought home. Many of our favourite dogs were brought home like this, and this batch was no different.

With some waterworks and lots of pleading, we were allowed to keep four of the puppies – one for each of us – while the rest were sent to a neighbour who was looking for pups.

But while warm snuffling puppies were one thing, the hounds from Hell in Uncle Oscar's house were rather more frightening. A few weeks later, Daddy had to visit Uncle Oscar and we tagged along with him. We took our school books with us so we could do our homework while the grown-ups chatted.

Uncle Oscar's house was an apartment on the first floor, with big sliding glass doors leading out onto a balcony. That evening the balcony was dark and the sliding doors were pulled shut against the stormy night outside. The living room was cosy and still, and we settled down around the coffee table to begin our homework.

Kuku sat with her back against the glass doors, rocking back and forth as she mugged up her multiplication tables. I happened to glance up at Kuku a short while later, and I saw something that made me blink and rub my eyes.

There in the darkness of the balcony, something moved behind the glass door. It was almost imperceptible, but there was definitely someone hiding out there.

I shouted for Daddy and Izzy jumped up to catch the thief red-handed. But before he could swing the doors open, Uncle Oscar came running through.

"It's not a thief, Izzy!" he bellowed, yanking him backwards just in time. "I've got two new dogs – Satan and Lucifer…"

"Satan and Lucifer?" Izzy looked at us with round eyes, suitably impressed. We named our puppies Fluffy or Sparkles or Snowy, but these names were much more interesting. "Can we play with them?"

"I don't think you should, you know. They're not used to children."

He switched on the lights in the balcony and we saw two giant black Dobermanns waiting outside. One of them was sitting right behind Kuku, separated by just a sheet of glass. It was staring at Kuku's small head, its lips drawn back to bare sharp white teeth. We promised Uncle Oscar not to open the doors or go anywhere near the glass.

Daddy came in just in time to hear the end of this. "Ha!" he scoffed. "You don't know these kids, Oscar. They'll play with any dog. They pick up strays all the time. They love dogs!"

"No! Wait! Don't open those doors. They're not very friendly yet. I just got them a month ago and I haven't been able to train them properly."

Satan and Lucifer paced back and forth, their lean bodies bristling with nervous energy. Their ears pointed backwards on their heads, and the small stub tails were unnaturally still. No happy wagging here. We could hear their sharp nails clicking on the floor as they patrolled the balcony.

"Nonsense! Here, kids, come here and put your hands out like I showed you. Let them see you don't mean any harm. You shouldn't let them smell your fear." Daddy strode over to the balcony and flung the doors open, ignoring Uncle Oscar's protests.

We heard Satan's growl emanating from the depths of his belly, a low ominous sound that we might have missed if our self-preservation instincts had not been tingling already. These were not dogs; they were man-eating beasts and we didn't want anything to do with either of them. The four of us drew together and moved as one to hoist Kuku, the smallest and juiciest of us, onto the sofa.

Daddy stretched his hand out and turned to look back at us. "Look, just let them sniff you once and they'll know you want to be friends. What's wrong with you? You're always crazy about dogs, all of you. See, you just have to hold your han…… Yeaaaargghhhhh!"

Lucifer slunk up in one smooth black move and sank his teeth into Daddy's upper thigh. The dog's lips snarled and his forehead wrinkled with the strength he put into the bite. Daddy howled and jerked back, but the dog hung on with sheer evil determination. We, Daddy's loyal children, jumped onto the sofa, screaming our heads off and pressing our backs against the wall, as Uncle Oscar rushed forth to pummel his dog on the back.

When he managed to separate dog from man, he pulled Daddy into the house and slammed the doors shut. The dogs hurled themselves at the glass, raging that their prey had been taken from them. Uncle Oscar stood by the door, his hand on the lock, issuing a string of ineffective commands at them. Finally they settled down, noses against the glass, their eyes following every movement that was made inside the room.

Daddy collapsed onto the sofa in a heap, and once we were sure that the fiends were locked out, we swarmed around him to examine the injury and assure him that he would live. Warm blood seeped from his wound, deep red against his black jeans. Daddy tried to smile and reassure us, but we couldn't tear our eyes away from the oozing blood.

Uncle Oscar hurried about, trailing cotton wool and trying to find his bottle of Dettol. The evening passed in a haze as Daddy patched himself up, drove with us to hospital to get his anti-rabies shot and a generous dose of painkillers, and then drove home.

That day marked the beginning of a deep and sustained dislike of Dobermanns, and the entire Khot family has never gone near one ever since.

CHAPTER TWO

The Honorary Khots

Because we grew up inside an old Fort, separated from the city and everyone who lived there, it felt like we lived in a bubble. Our life at home was very distinct from our school life and our friends there. This old bungalow, its overgrown garden, and the people who lived closest to us provided enough fodder for our imaginations, and we didn't need anything else.

We spent all our time together, separating only when we had to go to school for a few hours of the day. At lunch break, we met like old friends and exchanged news of all the things that had happened to us in those few hours. On weekends, we played together and when the time came for afternoon naps or bedtime stories, we squeezed into one big bed, wrestling and kicking and chattering until we fell asleep.

Daddy often told us we were like four new-born puppies, staying close to each other for warmth and happiest when we were together. And he wasn't wrong. We didn't like being separated and were extraordinarily clannish, reluctant to admit an outsider into our ranks. But there were a few friends who made it through and became so close to us that they were honorary members of our respective families.

Mahua was my best friend and soul sister. Our families had known each other for the last two generations and we had been invited to each other's birthday parties as babies, but it wasn't until we were ten years old that we grew close. Mahua saved me a place in the assembly line at school one day and we began to talk.

Ordinarily we wouldn't have made friends with someone as gentle as Mahua. She had a small head, skinny arms and legs, and big eyes with long lashes. She looked just like a mild-mannered bunny, and the four of us preferred boisterous games. But then one day Mahua risked her life (or at least her arm) to save our dog Rum, and we recognised that her soft bunny exterior hid a streak of reckless bravery and gritty rebellion.

She came over to lend me some school notes one day, and as we stood there chatting, the two of us saw Rum choking on a large piece of bone. His eyes were bulging and his body convulsing as he panicked, trying to draw a breath. Although he was our dog, I was too frightened to do anything, but Mahua couldn't bear the sight of his suffering.

She wrestled him down to the floor, put her thin fingers straight into those frothing jaws and past the chomping teeth to pull out the bone. She dragged him to his water bowl and made him drink, tossed the bone aside, wiped her hands on her corduroy skirt, and resumed her conversation with me, while the four of us gaped at her in admiration. She was instantly inducted into the Khot family after that.

Zayra and Aaliya Hani were the same age as Kuku and Ritu and lived in the bungalow next to ours. Their father, Dr. Zaheer Hani, was our family doctor and had been patient with every skinned knee, stomach upset, and viral flu that we'd had. Zayra and Aaliya went to the same school as we did, and our families had a standing arrangement throughout our school years, sharing school pick-ups and lunch drop-offs. Zayra and Aaliya became so much a part of our daily lives that we spent almost every day, all birthday parties, and all festivals with them.

Zayra and Aaliya were true children of a family of doctors. They were very fact-oriented and were not at all convinced about many of the odd things that happened in the Khot house. We told them how the Easter Bunny hid chocolates and eggs in our garden at Easter, but they were doubtful. They came running over at 7 am on Christmas morning in response to a breathless phone call, to see snowy footprints from Santa's boots on the ground. We stood around the footprints and looked at them with a challenge in our eyes, but they were disbelieving. In the face of our vociferous conviction, they lost some of their certainty, but were always uncertain. Somehow, despite all our differences, we managed to grow closer every year.

And the littlest member of the entourage was Pinky, Kuku's best friend, all of 6 years old. She was small for her age, but she was plucky and fun and always up for anything. We met her at the grand opening of a restaurant run by a family friend. The four of us were running wild through the lawns, powered by the dozens of fizzy drinks that we'd guzzled, when we stumbled upon a storeroom hidden under the stairs.

The room was shrouded in dark velvet curtains and had stacks of plastic garden chairs and tables lined up against the walls. The floor was covered with a fine layer of dust and the windows were grimy. Nobody would disturb us here. Izzy declared that it was a shame to waste the room and decided that we should swing on the chandelier. He calculated, with one eye squeezed shut, that if we climbed the curtains on the window and reached over, we would be able to reach the edge of the chandelier.

We decided that there was enough here to keep us entertained for the whole evening, and settled down to watch as Izzy began to climb the curtains. The room was musty and cool, and it was soon echoing with the sound of Izzy's grunts and the instructions we shouted up to him.

A short while later, the door creaked open and we spun around, expecting to be caught by a grown-up and thrown out. We stood blinking in the bright light coming into the darkened room from outside, but nobody was there. A row of chairs blocked our view of the door, but they were only about four feet high and surely we should have been able to see a grown-up standing there.

Kuku and Ritu shuffled closer together, just in case it was a ghost. Then the door slammed shut and small heels clicked on the floor. All we could see over the chairs was a high ponytail, bouncing towards us. The four of us, including Izzy who was dangling from the curtain with his mouth open, waited to see who it was.

The ponytail, adorned with a bow, rounded the last plastic chair and we saw Pinky for the first time. She was the shortest person we had ever met, and she wore a foaming pink dress that made her look even smaller. She looked at us speculatively, undisturbed by the boy in formal clothes hanging on a curtain. Only one detail caught her eye.

"Why aren't any of you wearing shoes?" she asked, pointing at our feet.

"So we can get a better grip on the curtains," explained Kuku helpfully. She nodded up at Izzy, who had his toes curled to grip the curtain, just like a monkey.

Pinky seemed to accept this and plopped down on the floor to peel off her shoes and socks. We went back to climbing curtains and had a roaring good time, even though we didn't manage to make it to the chandelier. Later that night, we discovered that Pinky could drink a whole glass of Thums Up, thump on her chest, and let out a tremendous burp. Although we usually only approved of each other, she was really beginning to win our admiration.

When the time came to go home, Pinky threw a fearsome tantrum and made so much noise, despite her diminutive size, that her parents allowed her to come home with us for the weekend. It turned out that our parents knew each other, although this was hardly a surprise in a place like Belgaum. From that day onwards, Pinky became another fixture in our house.

CHAPTER THREE

An Egyptian Mummy in Fort

Back in the 80s and 90s, many of those who had left Belgaum for education or work began to return, leaving behind big cities and foreign shores in search of a better quality of life. Some moved back for the fresh air, the pleasant weather, and the relaxed pace. Some moved back as parents, wanting their children to play with animals and dance in the grass with bare feet, just like they had when they were kids. Some moved back to be with ageing parents and chose to stay on long after those parents were looking down at them from the heavens.

Belgaum became a fun, vibrant place for these young couples with their noisy offspring. Most homes we visited had gardens or terraces, and people hosted al fresco picnics, birthday parties on the lawns, and tandoori nights under shimmering skies.

We loved outdoor dinner parties, because it gave us the run of the house and an evening of unsupervised bliss. We knew that once the grown-ups had set up their bars and ice boxes, they didn't worry too much what we were up to. Tight knots of marauding kids roamed about, looking for bottles of Thums Up or Fanta, or keeping an eye on the cake or ice-cream or *gulab jamuns* that were calling out our names. We were allowed to stay up late, play games in dark gardens, and watch Disney movies even on school nights.

Some of my earliest memories are of our weekly party on Amol Kaka's terrace. Amol Kaka had a big hearty laugh and a gentle heart, and was my favourite uncle on Daddy's side. He had fought like a lion in his Army days, and we loved to pester him for his stories. After he retired, he settled in Belgaum with his wife, Janhavi Kaki. They were both always ready to show us a magic trick or tell us a joke, and he never blinked when we held rowdy races on the stairs of his house, with his sons, our cousins.

In those days, Doordarshan was the only television channel everyone had, and we watched whatever was on. Once a week, late at night, all the grown-ups of our family met at Amol Kaka's house to watch *The Hound of the Baskervilles* on Doordarshan. By the time we got there in the evening, Amol Kaka had laid out mattresses on the terrace, carried the television up and connected the antenna, and cooked a big tub of mutton curry.

The grown-ups chatted and laughed and poured drinks, while the kids tore about on the terrace until it was time for dinner. We devoured plates of mutton curry and rice, and then lay on those mattresses under the stars, listening to the comforting clinking of glasses and the murmur of voices. We fell asleep in the laps of anyone who was nearby, and everyone patted us to sleep or held a soft hand over our ears if the vicious hound was barking. We never even knew when we were carried home and tucked into bed.

But as we grew older, the four of us were put to work at a party, especially if it was arranged at our house. Most of our parties were held in the garden, where there was space for a bonfire and a *tandoor* or barbecue grill, as well as plenty of comfortable seating.

On one such night, Izzy and I were dutifully sprinkling rose petals into the light-up fountain on the food table. Daddy liked to have 'atmospherics' at our parties, so we've always had a collection of electric fountains, groovy lava lamps, or strings of twinkling fairy lights to be draped in trees.

Izzy and I were having a heated discussion about our Big Plan, eyes darting about to make sure nobody was listening. It was a big party and we had a big garden. We knew nobody would bother about us once the party started, and we had formulated a scheme that would take appropriate advantage of this freedom.

Mahua was on her way over already, so I was keen to finish up my part of the work. Kuku had made a phone call all by herself to invite Pinky. Zayra and Aaliya were already here, toiling along with the smallies to lay out the forks and spoons on the party tables. As glamorous as it was to be honorary family members at each other's homes, we were all also roped in to do the chores that came up in anyone's house.

The smallies urged Izzy to tell them about the Big Plan again and Izzy was delighted to do so. On a recent tidying-up session that we had been forced to do, we had discovered a terrifying mask of an Egyptian Mummy. It had a rotting bandaged face, gaping black holes for the eyes, and a demonic smile. Every time we looked at it, we shuddered and quickly turned it over.

We also unearthed a long white robe with a hood, a souvenir from Saudi Arabia that Daddy and Mummy had brought home from their travels in the '70s. It was six feet long, so we had to hold it up when we walked, but the length hid our hands and feet and made it look like we're floating. It looked like it had been made to use with the mask.

At night, the roads of the Fort were shrouded in darkness, with towering trees blocking out the streetlamps and the moonlight. People from Belgaum city believed that ghosts and spirits roamed the Fort freely after dusk, and while the families that lived inside knew better, we didn't bother to dispel the rumours. We liked the peace and solitude of our quiet surroundings. Some of us may have even added a few stories of our own.

It was easy to believe the rumours. By the time dusk fell, owls hooted from the treetops, the white painted walls of the *dargah* gleamed in the dim light, and strange creatures rustled in the grass. If you asked rickshaw drivers from the city to take you into the Fort after 7 o'clock in the evening, they'd look at you like you were crazy, click their tongue against their teeth and drive off shaking their heads.

But there were always a few brave souls who were tempted by the shortcut to the other side of the city. They ventured through the stone gateways of the Fort, always a little jumpy while they were inside. That small prickle of fear primed them for the fright we had planned.

The night was dark and perfect for scaring a few unsuspecting strangers. As the evening progressed, the stars aligned to make it a memorable evening. Mahua and Pinky had arrived, and the grown-ups were pouring their second 'not-for-kids' drinks. All of us had consumed enough chips and sugary drinks to feel reckless and daring, and Izzy and I were ready to reveal the evening's entertainment.

Once we had shown Mahua and Pinky the mask, we began to explain out the plan. Izzy desperately wanted the Egyptian Mummy to wave a swashbuckling sword, but the best we could do was steal some knives from the kitchen. Clutching the mask and the robes under our shirts, we pushed through the hedge and filed out into the road, the knives gleaming as they sliced through the air.

As the first-born, I decided I would get the first turn. I slipped the robe over my head, pulled the mask on, and grasped the two knives tight. Mahua shivered at the sight of me and gave me a thumbs up. Pinky, Aaliya, and Kuku (on lookout duty because they were too short for the robe) hissed to warn us that the first victim was approaching, and we quickly took up our positions.

A solo cyclist appeared, pedalling at a leisurely pace along the quiet road. All he could hear was the hooting of owls and the twanging of crickets. Even the music and lights from our party were muted and far away. The cool night air was crisp and refreshing, and his pedals creaked softly.

"Wheyaaaaaaaaaarggghhhh" I yelled, leaping out from the bushes into his path. The man squawked and wobbled on his cycle as he swerved to avoid me. I ran beside him, bellowing incoherently and making stabbing gestures with my knives. The man pumped his knees and sped off into the darkness, glancing over his shoulder with wild and terrified eyes. I chased him to the corner and then stopped, laughing uncontrollably behind the mask. When I got back to the bushes, everyone had collapsed with delight.

We couldn't have expected a better reaction, and we were eager to do the next round. Mahua went next, pushing aside Izzy who was begging for his turn. She pulled the robe over her head and slipped the mask on. Her big eyes rolled about in the dark eye sockets of the mask, and we approved the effect and settled down in the bushes to wait.

It was a longer wait this time, but just as we were growing tired of the buzzing mosquitoes, we heard a moped in the distance. A couple on a bike appeared in view, riding slowly and whispering sweet nothings to each other. Mahua cackled inside her mask and we held our breath. As the bike approached, we pushed her to jump out but she ignored our prodding fingers, waiting instead for it to go past.

Once they were about 20 feet away, Mahua ran out on silent feet towards them, letting out a long and gruesome howl. "Aaaaaaaoooooooooaaagghhh"

The girl on the bike snapped her head around. Her eyes popped when she saw the ghoul that was rushing towards them. She shrieked and began pounding on her lover's back, pulling her legs up as if she wanted to climb over him. He didn't understand what she was screaming, but he responded promptly to the pounding, revving his bike so hard that their necks snapped backwards as they shot forth.

Mahua ran as fast as she could, holding her robe up with one hand and waving the knife in a horrifying way. The girl gabbled her prayers out loud, hiding her face and holding on to her boyfriend's back while he tried to turn the corner. His bike skidded on some gravel and for a few dreadful seconds it slewed sideways. As the girl called out to her ancestors to protect her, her suitor scrabbled his feet desperately to maintain his balance, managing to make the turn and stay upright.

But the sight proved too much for Mahua. She stopped to rest her hands on her knees, choking with laughter behind the mask and letting the couple ride off as fast as the bike would go. We emerged from the bushes clapping and laughing, and Mahua walked back like a conquering hero.

CHAPTER FOUR

Catching Crabs for Dinner

While Belgaum enjoyed the shimmering summer days of April and May, a few hundred kilometres away from us, large monsoon clouds were fast approaching. Trapped by the Western Ghats, the clouds assembled overhead, swelling and becoming darker as each day went by.

The grown-ups looked at the skies and exchanged knowledgeable opinions about when it would rain. We unpacked our raincoats and washed off the talcum powder that had been dusted into the folds. Grim clouds gathered overhead and the air felt static and heavy. The summer heat turned into a suffocating humidity that made our faces sticky. As the days stretched into weeks, it felt like we were all holding our breath and waiting for something.

And then one day, usually in the afternoon, the sky would split open and empty an ocean upon us. It began with fat droplets, giving us time to rush about pulling clothes off the lines. As the winds began to howl around our bungalow, the coconut trees swayed dangerously, buffeted by gusts of rain.

We unplugged the television and the refrigerator to protect them from surges in the voltage, and dived under our blankets for a nap, always a little shocked at the first violent rainfall of the season. Lightning darted across the sky, and ominous rumbles from above announced the arrival of the rain gods.

Our tiled roof sprang leaks all over the house and Kuku and Ritu were sent to place buckets and saucepans under each leak to collect the water. For the next three months, our daily lives played out against the soundtrack of raindrops pinging in steel vessels.

Inside our bungalow, the forces of nature took over like a mad conductor directing a frenzied orchestra. Our garden, overgrown and wild at the best of times, began to hum with the throbbing of life. If you stood barefoot on the soil, you could almost feel the tender green shoots unfurling under the ground and pushing up against the soles of your feet. The trees danced like whirling dervishes, spreading branches wide to catch every sparkling droplet. Creepers twirled and swayed as they stretched upwards to the skies.

One of the best things about living in Belgaum was our proximity to nature. We were never more than half an hour away from sprawling meadows and forests so thick that you could barely see the sun. Every weekend, Daddy took us out into the wild, sending us rappelling over unknown cliffs, scaling up the mossy rocks beside thundering waterfalls, or swimming in limpid lakes. We looked forward to our nature rambles all year round, but it was in the monsoon that the land around us burst into truly spectacular life.

We made the most of our monsoon months, heading out for rainy treks and waterfall swims as often as we could, but the weekends that really excited us were our crabbing expeditions. Daddy took us out on the rainiest weekends of the year to the hills nearby, where water gushed in streams under our feet. Each of us each carried a small bucket and waded through the slush, looking for crabs darting in the rivulets.

The grown-ups who accompanied us chattered about crab curry with soft *pao* or fluffy steamed rice on the side. We loved crab curry, but for us, the kids who were pouncing on puddles and turning our faces up to the raindrops, chasing the crabs was infinitely more fun than eating them.

To catch a crab, you have to be very quick and very sure-footed. You approach it from behind, keeping a safe distance from those snapping pincers. One finger on top of the shell to hold it down, and the thumb under it, "lifting it up from its bum" as Pinky and Kuku liked to say, and you lift it and drop it into your bucket.

Pinky and Kuku usually worked together, hitching up their skirts and raincoats and crouching close to the ground, scuttling sideways just like the crabs they were chasing. Ritu wandered over every now and then to see how many crabs they had in their bucket, but she was a crack crab-catcher and enjoyed working on her own. Izzy and I preferred to cover more ground, ranging far and wide to look for the bigger pools where the bigger crabs lived.

On the way back, we emptied our buckets into a large tub in the back of the Sumo, and gloated over our catch – dozens of brown crabs waiting for Tulsi Bai's tasty curry. All the smallest members of the group were squeezed in around the tub to make sure the crabs didn't climb out on the 45-minute drive back home. While Daddy drove us back, the crabs built towers on each other's backs, swarming up the sides of the tub to escape.

Every year, the smallies named all the crabs, starting with Crabby, Pinchy, Browny, and then Crabby I, Crabby, II and so on. Nobody knew which crab was which, but as none of these creatures had any recognizable personality traits except a tendency to scuttle, it didn't matter. The smallies spent the drive focused on the tub, plucking crabs off their clothes and off the floor, knocking back the towers with squeals, and shouting reports to all of us about what the crabs were doing.

By the time we got home, all of us were so deeply invested in the efforts of Crabby, Browny and Pinchy that we didn't want to see them floating in our curry.

Daddy and Kanappa made a big show of inspecting the crabs while we stood by with sinking hearts. When they declared that the crabs were too small and would have to be put in the well for a few weeks to grow bigger, we breathed a sigh of relief. Tulsi Bai made us a big bowl of *khichdi* instead, and we ate that just as happily.

Over the years, our well has been filled with many generations of Pinchies, Brownies and Crabbies, and they have all grown as large as our palms. In the monsoon, the well overflows and the odd crab can sometimes be spotted scurrying across the road outside our garden, but none have ever been served on our plates.

CHAPTER FIVE

Meet Mr. Waffles

The four of us idled beside the gate of our house, waiting for a glimpse of the rickshaw that would bring Veena Tai from the station. Kuku and Ritu sat on a rock, propping their chins on their hands, with Eclipse pirouetting at their feet, asking for attention. Rum and Raisin pranced along beside Izzy as he paced up and down practising his spin-bowling move. We wanted to be the first to greet Veena Tai and get one of her warm hugs, but we were also competing to race inside and announce to Aji that her darling daughter had arrived.

Veena Tai was Daddy's big sister, and all through our childhood, she visited a few times a year to meet Aji and help her organise and rearrange mountains of our clothes, toys, and books. We always looked forward to her visit because she brought a bag full of goodies for us: homemade mayonnaise and ketchup, baked beans, jams of all kinds, cakes and *halwa*, and clothes that she had made. It was like the bottomless bag that Mary Poppins owned, with pianos and lamp-posts stored inside.

We were always a little worried about sustaining our best behaviour for the duration of Veena Tai's visits. She had been a teacher and a principal all her working life, and this appeared to have given her magical powers. Although she spent hours chatting peaceably with Aji, snipping and stitching at a pile of our clothes that needed repair, she didn't have to move from her chair to know what we were doing in the room at the far end of the house.

If Kuku was wiggling in her chair, she sent her off to the toilet to "check if anything wanted to come out", and it usually did.

If Izzy was very quiet for a long time, she called out to ask him what he was doing. Izzy usually had a thieving hand in the chocolate box or was holding Ritu's head in a vice-like grip in the crook of his elbow. He'd jump, call back in his most innocent voice to say that he was reading, and then skulk off on soft feet. When Veena Tai told us she had eyes behind her head, we didn't doubt it for even a second.

Daddy and Veena Tai shared many traits: they were both sharply intelligent and did not tolerate idiocy, both had an insatiable sweet tooth, and both walked with quick, impatient strides. They were also the best story-tellers we knew, and when Veena Tai was in town, she took over the story-telling duties from Daddy. We listened open-mouthed to tales of what she and Daddy did when they were little, how our grandfather caught a tiger, how her cats almost got bitten by a snake, and what happens to little children who don't eat the food on their plate.

Last time Veena Tai visited, she told us a story about a very smart rabbit and from that day on, I had begged Daddy to get us one. Now that we finally had one, I couldn't wait for Veena Tai to arrive so that I could show him to her.

It had been almost impossible to find a rabbit in Belgaum because so few people kept them as pets. Then one day on the way back from school, Daddy stopped to meet Uncle Srikanth, who lived inside the Fort, not far from our house. While he chatted inside, we hopped out of the Sumo and began scouting the garden for something interesting to do.

It was a drizzly, mosquito-buzzy kind of evening, and we were hungry and cranky and couldn't wait to get home to our evening tea and biscuits. But we forgot all about that when we stumbled upon a ramshackle hen coop by the outhouse, with a fat white rabbit inside. His startlingly white fur stood out even in the grey of the dusk and for a few seconds, we couldn't believe our eyes.

We squatted by the coop and made the usual *Pss Pss Tsk Tsk* sounds that we used to communicate with our cats and dogs, but the rabbit didn't respond. He looked miserable, stuck in the damp wooden shell of a cage which was too small for him to even turn around in. We ripped up grass from nearby and tried to push it through the cage to feed him, but he just turned his head away.

A rabbit is so fragile that even unexpected loud noises like firecrackers or dogs barking can stop its heart. In all the bungalows of the Fort, there were dogs that barked and raced about all night, and the dogs of this bungalow were no different. We knew they were stopping by occasionally to sniff and growl menacingly at the rabbit at night and realised how lonely and terrified he must be.

Just when we had worked ourselves into a fury about this poor rabbit's awful life, the owner showed up, red-eyed and unsteady on his feet. We turned on him and reproached him in our broken Marathi and Hindi and convent-educated English. He tried to focus his eyes and mumbled that it wasn't really lonely because he had just brought it from the farm where it lived with dozens of other rabbits.

Izzy bounced up at this and began to accuse him of wanting to eat it and that we would bring the police to catch him. The man's face began to turn purple with rage and he stepped forward in an unpleasantly threatening manner. Daddy turned the corner looking for us and was just in time to hear the string of unsavoury words that the man unleashed.

A heated exchange followed, and Daddy called the man *gadhe ki aulad*, which was our favourite bad word. The man told Daddy if we liked the rabbit so much, we might as well buy it and get out. With cries of joy, we fell upon the cage, unhooked it, and gathered the rabbit lovingly into our arms. Daddy had not really intended this, but it was too late to get out of it now.

We balanced the rabbit between us and looked beseechingly at Daddy. The rabbit, ensconced in the eight arms of his new family, blinked calmly and twitched his nose. The owner beamed, burped, scratched his belly with his grimy fingers, and quoted his price for the rabbit. It was Daddy's turn to mutter some bad words, but he riffled through his pockets for cash with bad grace.

The rabbit sat on my lap as we drove home. All the way back, Daddy warned us that we would have to feed and clean the rabbit and not let our new pet add to Kanappa's work. Having heard all this before, we nodded and made the obedient sounds he expected, while the smallies leaned over each other to stroke the rabbit and coo at him. He waggled his big ears happily and gave a tiny sigh. In the five minutes it took to get home, I had fallen deeply in love.

The rabbit was a Californian White, with snow white fur, ruby red eyes, a fat bum, and a cheeky bobtail. We couldn't take our eyes off him. We named him Mr. Waffles, and although Daddy and Kanappa built a shelter for him in the garden, none of us could bear to leave him alone in the dark night. So we booted Eclipse out of our bedroom, locked all our doors, and Mr. Waffles went from staying in a decaying cage in the outhouse to sleeping in our cosy bedroom every night.

We tried to get him to sleep inside our bed with us like a cat, but he preferred to be outside the mosquito net. At night, he hopped over and stood on his hind legs at our bed to watch us, not wanting to let us out of his sight. Every time he stood up, the four of us sat up in bed to talk to him. Daddy finally found a creative solution to this, and placed a chair next to the bed and draped his dressing gown over it to form a shelter. Mr. Waffles hopped up to sit on the chair, his hind paws splayed out behind him like frog legs, and watched over us all night as we slept.

Mr. Waffles was the smartest rabbit we had ever seen. On his first day in our house, he saw one of us on the potty and realised what the bathroom was for. After that, he began to use the corner near the drain-hole as his own toilet, so it was easy to clean. He sat on our laps or dozed on my desk while I wrestled with geometry and algebra. He hopped up to us when we came back from school, raising his paws so he could be lifted up and petted and kissed after our long separation.

The rest of our family didn't appreciate our rabbit as much as we did. Kanappa told us often that rabbit curry was a delicacy in the villages around Belgaum, then scurried off, cackling at our indignant protests. To the utmost annoyance of Aji and Tulsi Bai, we discovered that Mr. Waffles loved coriander and lettuce. Frequent sorties were made into the fridge under the pretext of drinking milk or cold water, only to smuggle away the choicest vegetables to feed our new beloved. Mr. Waffles grew so heavy and so fat that Kuku had to use both arms and huff and puff to lift him up.

And now Veena Tai was visiting. Every time she arrived, we trotted out all our new pets, new drawings and prize certificates, new tooth gaps, new scars and new friends for her to see. She *oohed* and *aahed* in the appropriate places, encouraged or sympathised when necessary, took the time to listen to our breathless and disjointed stories, and was altogether a grand audience for us.

On this visit, I couldn't wait to show her Mr. Waffles. I pointed out Mr. Waffles' many beautiful features and Veena Tai duly appreciated them all. We showed her how he licked all the sugar off a jujube before he ate it, and how he jumped over obstacles if we lined them up and she was suitably impressed.

But about a week into her visit, Veena Tai noticed that Mr. Waffles was plucking fur off his belly and storing it in corners. We worried about him for hours, trying to tempt him with tomato slices and coriander sprigs, all of which disappeared into his round belly. Kanappa laughed and told us we were seasoning him just perfectly for a tandoori dinner and then sheepishly hurried away when the torrents of tears began, leaving Veena Tai to console us and put us to bed.

Kuku, who was deeply influenced by her favourite nun in school, offered to pray for Mr. Waffles' health, so Veena Tai bowed her head and joined us. It appeared that the Lord worked a miracle that night, because Veena Tai woke us up very early with a big smile. She whispered that Mr. Waffles had a surprise for us and we stumbled out of our blankets to follow her.

There he was, lying on his side behind a box of old sweaters, with a pile of small pink babies next to him. Our Mr. Waffles wasn't a Mister; he was a Mrs! We squealed and fell to the floor around the babies, whispering in delight. The babies looked just like little mice, pink and furless, with closed eyes.

By the time Veena Tai's visit came to an end, we had a brood of furry baby bunnies to play with. We spent all our time after school with the rabbits, telling them stories and choosing and discarding names. Aji and Tulsi Bai resigned themselves to a lifetime of feeding expensive vegetables to the rabbits, and Kanappa, on Veena Tai's strict instructions, held his tongue about any culinary suggestions.

It was too late to change names, so for the rest of her life, she remained Mr. Waffles.

As Mr. Waffles grew into the fat matriarch of a fast-multiplying brood, she also became immune to the sounds of Rum and Raisin. Her sturdy descendants took a cue from her, and by the time we were forced by Aji to move the entire bunny family into the hutch in our garden, they didn't blink an eye at the raucous barking.

CHAPTER SIX

Fairies in the Tree House

"Baby! Wake up! Wake up!"

I rolled over in my blankets, mumbling into the night. We had gone to bed hours ago, and I couldn't imagine why Daddy was waking me up now. Surely it wasn't time for school yet.

"Wake up! The fairies are here. They're in your tree house."

I sat bolt upright up in bed, wide awake. The room was dark, except for the red glow of our night light. Daddy stood outside the mosquito net in his dressing gown, with his newspaper still in his hand. Aji was fast asleep in her room next to us, and Izzy snored in the top bunk of the bunk bed.

"Are you sure, Daddy?"

"What do you mean?" he sputtered. "Of course I'm sure! I just heard them. Get the smallies and come out quick, or else we'll miss them." And with that, Daddy turned and disappeared.

I fumbled around for Kuku and Ritu. Kuku slept next to me, and every night, she managed to rotate in bed, waking up in the morning with her feet on the pillow. I found Kuku's ankle and shook her awake, then rummaged through the mosquito net to wake up Ritu.

We had a bunk bed, complete with ladder, lined up beside our double bed. Ritu slept in the lower bunk and Izzy slept on top. Daddy slept on the far edge of the double bed to protect us from ghosts and from falling off the edge.

"The fairies are having a party in the tree-house" I hissed. Ritu woke up quickly and thumped her palm under Izzy's bunk to wake him up. He stopped snoring immediately, always a light (but noisy) sleeper, and all of us tumbled out of bed.

Daddy made sure we had our slippers and sweaters on before leading us out into the dark garden. Rum and Raisin wagged their tails and raced up to greet us, puzzled but thrilled to be reunited with us at this hour of the night. From behind them, emerging from the pile of gunny sacks they slept in, our four puppies gambolled up, looking for snacks. Eclipse unfurled from the shadows that completely camouflaged his black fur and stalked up to see what was happening. All of us spent a few seconds calming our clan.

"Don't make any noise, you hear? The fairies are very shy creatures and they'll fly away if they even suspect that we're watching them." Daddy looked at us in the moonlight, trying to make sure we understood. He shot a pointed look at Kuku, liable to squeal in her excitement, and she nodded obediently, saucer-eyed with anticipation.

"Okay. Come on then. And don't trip on the dogs like last time." Daddy led the way around the side of the house. We walked under the row of coconut trees on soft feet, Daddy first, with a restraining hand on Izzy's shoulder. Ritu and Kuku walked with each other, with the cat cradled on Ritu's shoulder. I followed, bringing up the rear, while Rum and Raisin ran in circles around us, shepherding us without knowing where we were headed.

It was a chilly night and the moon was full. The moonlight burnished the trunks of the coconut trees and cast a silvery glow over the garden. Our *raat ki rani* bush was sprinkled with thousands of white blossoms that sent an intoxicating sweet fragrance into the crisp air. The crickets filled the night with their strange music. It was the perfect night for a fairy tea party.

Daddy stopped at the corner and raised a hand to tell us to wait. Kuku and Ritu missed the signal, bumped into Daddy and stopped. We waited, straining to see fairies in the darkness or to hear their tinkling voices, but all we heard were the crickets.

"You must have made too much noise" admonished Daddy. He crept closer to the tree house followed by us, Izzy doing his best Pink Panther walk on his toes and all of us following suit. When we reached the chikoo tree, it was silent. We looked around expectantly for a few minutes and then turned to Daddy, downcast. There was no glow from magical fairy wings, no glitter sprinkling down into our faces, and no new fairy friends to make.

"Come here, Mahi," Dad said. "We must have just missed them. Look inside the tree-house and see if they left anything."

I put the puppies down and he hoisted me up on his shoulders. The tree house was about 6 feet high, and we usually climbed the tree to get into it. But Daddy lifted me up so I could grab the railings and pull myself over the edge of it to look inside.

"Daddy, there's food here!" I was astonished.

"What? What food?"

"It's FAIRY FOOD."

"No! Don't be silly. The fairies wouldn't leave any clues behind like that. The four of you must have left it there today. I told you not to eat anything up there or the ants will start visiting every day."

"No, Daddy, no no! We didn't even come up here today. It's fairy food! Look!" I held up the remnants of a cupcake that I know we hadn't eaten.

By now, the smallies were hopping from one leg to the other with excitement. Izzy pulled himself free from Daddy's hand and tore up the tree, climbing like a monkey into the treehouse. Daddy hoisted Kuku and Ritu up and I pulled them over.

"Look, Daddy, look! A bit of bread!"

"Daddy, Daddy! A half-eaten banana."

"Daddy, how come we always miss them? I want to see them so bad."

"Well, all of you take so much time to get ready, and you make so much noise. I could hear them from all the way inside the house before I woke you up. They must have flown away just seconds before you arrived. Next time, we'll have to be faster and quieter."

We spent half an hour there, talking down from the tree house to Daddy, who stood in the moonlight in his blue dressing gown, arms akimbo, laughing up at us. Finally, it was time to go back to our warm beds and blankets, and we promised ourselves we would be on time to see them next time.

In the year after we lost our mother, the four of us had frequent nightmares for many months. After waking up crying or being woken up by whoever was having a bad dream, we dreaded bedtime. Daddy tried reading to us till we fell asleep, keeping a night lamp on, and stayed awake long into the night to keep an eye on us.

But the nightmares didn't stop and we made endless requests for another glass of water or one last trip to the toilet. And so Daddy devised all kinds of exciting and magical plans for our nights, giving us something fun to look forward to when we drifted off to the land of Nod.

Long after we had brushed our teeth and gone to sleep, he would throw open the mosquito net and declare a Midnight Ice-Cream Party, while we scrambled up and rubbed the sleep from our eyes. We devoured bowls of ice-cream in bed, serving second helpings and giggling at silly jokes, before going back to sleep without brushing our teeth. It was our biggest thrill and the ice-cream always tasted better at midnight.

When the fairy tea parties started taking place in our tree-house, the four of us were delirious with excitement. We often asked Daddy if today was the day, but the parties only took place when the moon was full. Somehow, we were always too late to catch the fairies at their party, but we always found bits of the food they left behind.

CHAPTER SEVEN

Sundays are for Dynamite Fishing

A long weekend was coming up, and Daddy announced that we were going fishing before the monsoon began. The four of us grimaced at each other. We knew what that meant: a boring afternoon of standing by the river, coming home with nothing but a few minnows to show for all our effort.

The first time we went fishing, we had been terribly excited. For all our weekend expeditions, we knew the drill. Daddy liked an early start, so instead of waking Tulsi Bai up to make tea and breakfast for us, we made it ourselves. Between the four of us, aged 6 to 11, we could make tea, fill up two thermos flasks, and slap some sandwiches together.

Daddy paced about wiping the windshield, checking the brakes and the petrol, and throwing spares into the back of the Sumo. But before we left on our first fishing trip, we tiptoed off to Tulsi Bai's house to inform her that we'd bring back a bucket of fish for her to fry for our dinner.

All the way to the river, Daddy lectured us about how fishing was an art and would teach us patience, and how we would feel a sense of accomplishment. But after four hours of casting our lines and catching nothing, we were not feeling very enthused about this sport. A few of the uncles who had come with us gave up and sat down to enjoy a second cup of tea, and Daddy wasn't feeling very patient himself.

We returned that evening with crestfallen faces and three measly fish that were already starting to stink. Luckily, Aji had had the forethought to send Kanappa to the market to buy fish, so we still got our fried fish dinner but it didn't taste the same. After our second attempt at fishing with the same results, Daddy wasn't feeling particularly patient or introspective either, and so the Khot family quietly gave up on fishing.

Until Uncle John mentioned *dynamite fishing*.

Uncle John came from a fishing village on the banks of the river, but had moved to Belgaum a few years ago to run a transport business, bringing vegetables from the farms to the city. He was also a bit of a local fixer and dabbled in some grey areas of the law, but we loved visiting his shop because he gave us pieces of sugarcane to chew on while he chatted with Daddy. He lived in a small room behind his shop, where he sold homemade pickles and oil.

When he heard about our disappointment, he told us that when the fishing was bad and the money ran low, the locals used dynamite to catch fish. We wanted to know everything about this thrilling sport, but finally, after patiently answering dozens of our questions, he threw his hands up and invited us to go with him next time so we could see for ourselves.

Two weeks later, he called us. He was going to take the dynamite from Belgaum that weekend, and if we were still interested, we could go with him and watch. He told us not to tell anyone, and we promised. But we couldn't control our excitement and by the time Sunday came around, we were a group of 25 adults and 10 kids. Church plans, family outings, extra tuition classes – all were cancelled. Nobody said no to dynamite fishing.

A box of locally made dynamite was carefully placed in the back of the Sumo, and the smallies – Kuku, Ritu, and Pinky – were checked for matches and then seated on top. Izzy was put in the front seat, between Daddy and Uncle John, because he couldn't keep his hands away from the dynamite. He had to content himself with yelling at the smallies not to fart into the box or else the whole car would explode.

The villagers were gathered in a group on the banks of the river that had defeated us twice before. They were slightly taken aback at the size of our group and looked warily at us as we trooped by, dressed in our colourful weekend clothes, carrying flasks of tea and sandwiches. The authorities frowned on dynamite fishing and they didn't want to attract undue attention. Uncle John loped over to them and after an animated discussion, told us to walk down the river some distance away.

We did as instructed and settled down to wait for the show to begin. Except for Izzy, who ambled over and stood right next to the villagers. This was the most exciting event to happen in his year, and he wanted to be close enough to catch all the action. He was particularly fascinated by Sanju, the skinny boy who was lugging a sling bag and a coil of rope over his shoulder, preparing to go into the water. Izzy pestered him and the villagers to let him join too, and they wagged their heads and gesticulated wildly in refusal.

The river was in full spate and Izzy, at 9 years, would be tossed about like a shrimp in it. But he had a curious face and bright eyes and was missing a front tooth, and even the guarded villagers couldn't resist his enthusiasm. After much pleading, Daddy gave in and nodded to Uncle John, who was grinning nearby.

Someone ran back to the village and returned with the inflatable tube from an old truck tyre. They put Izzy into it and tied him to it so he wouldn't slip under in his excitement. The tube was tied to a tree so he couldn't go deeper than the edges of the river, and he was given strict instructions to wait until he was told to go in.

The moment of truth arrived. A fisherman from the village took the dynamite and jogged a few minutes along the river so he was upstream of us. We saw him light the dynamite carefully; a brief flame flared, and he arced his arm up and lobbed the stick into the middle of the river. Breathless silence. *Had the dynamite been extinguished in the water?*

And then there was a muted BOOM in the water. A bubble, almost 6 feet in diameter, rose to the surface. We waited and watched. Izzy stood by the side of the river, rocking on his heels and waiting to dive in.

Just in front of us, downstream from the explosion, a large silver fish appeared on the surface, stunned from the explosion. Then another popped up. And then another. Sanju tightened the rope around his waist and slipped into the river, striking out towards the fish. Izzy howled in triumph and waddled in, plucking his knees up to get through the sludgy mud and holding the tyre up around him.

Sanju stuffed fish into his bag and we cheered him on, screaming as more and more fish, each one longer than his forearm, floated to the surface. Izzy thrashed desperately on the edges of the river, longing to get closer, and it seemed as if the heavens took pity on him. A few of the smaller fish bobbed up near him, and without hesitating, he grabbed them and shoved them into his pockets.

He bawled to the villagers to get ready as he paddled back with his loot. When he emerged from the river, his shorts were hopping with the flip-flopping fish, and Izzy was squirming to stop their tails from tickling his ribs.

The villagers laughed and helped him empty his pockets. They grabbed the flopping fish by the tails and slipped them into buckets of river water lined up under the cover of the trees. By afternoon, Sanju had filled eight buckets of fish and Izzy had managed to bring back quite a few small ones.

The fishermen were happy with their loot and set about dividing the buckets between themselves. Sanju generously offered Izzy some fish, but Daddy and Uncle John declined, to our great regret. We were looking forward to showing off the big fish to Tulsi Bai and Aji, and certainly didn't want to return empty-handed again.

On our way back, Mahua and I hesitantly asked Uncle John if the dynamite fishing was bad for the environment. We were just old enough to have heard about the ozone hole and Greenpeace, and were developing a strong opinion about what man was doing to the environment. We were sure that the grown-ups in our life would never do anything bad, but the morning's activities seemed unfair to the fish.

Uncle John took us to a small cafe run by a lady in the village, where he bought all of us plates of *idli* with *sambar* poured over. While we sat there, our fringes curling in the aromatic steam rising from the bowls, he explained to us kindly that the dynamite fishing wasn't for sport. If Sanju hadn't gone home with fish today, he wouldn't have had any money to buy food tomorrow. That's why, even though it wasn't legal, Uncle John paid for and transported dynamite from the city to the village.

We didn't learn patience or introspection that day, but we learned a lot about generosity. Uncle John owned four shirts and two pairs of trousers, and slept in a room barely big enough to fit a single bed, but he did more for the struggling fishermen of his village than anyone could guess. And he did it with a bang!

CHAPTER EIGHT

Nobody Likes the New Governess

After hearing about some of our more dangerous pranks and stopping wrestling matches that left us scarred and scratched, Daddy began to think that we were running a little too wild. He decided that what we needed was a governess to teach us manners and discipline.

We were not enthusiastic about this idea and insisted that we could look after ourselves. Having seen *The Sound of Music* many times, we knew what to expect. A governess would make us sing songs and wear clothes made from old curtains, and then she would weasel her way into the family and marry Daddy. But Aji agreed with Daddy and as nobody asked us for our opinion, or listened when we gave it, which we did (vehemently), Project Governess was put into action.

After weeks of making enquiries, someone at the local church recommended a lovely old lady named Martha. She had been a school teacher in Goa, and was recently widowed, with grown-up children who lived abroad. Phone calls were made and decisions were made. The very next Sunday, Daddy and all four of us packed into the Sumo with enough sunglasses, flasks of tea, and snacks to sustain us through an apocalypse, and drove down to Goa to pick her up.

Daddy had already told her about us, and like a good Christian she was filled with sympathy for these poor motherless mites. However, we didn't want anyone's sympathy, and when she emerged from her home with tears in her rheumy old eyes and tried to gather us together in a group hug, we instantly disliked her.

On the drive back to Belgaum, she told us she had come up with lovely nicknames for us. From now on, Mahi would be Tinkerbell, Izzy would be Hero, Ritu would be Rosebud, and Kuku would be Pixie. Izzy and I rolled our eyes at each other and informed her that we already had nicknames: Mahi was Mahi Bear, Izzy was Jean Claude, Ritu was Sally Wrigglesworth, and Kuku was Fatty or Wallie.

Martha was not impressed with these names but tactfully decided to let it go. She focussed instead on explaining to Daddy how difficult her financial situation had been and how she was so happy to be able to help.

We sat in the back of the Sumo sniggering while Ritu flicked tiny biscuit crumbs into Martha's grey hair. She smelled strongly of tobacco and wine, but that didn't bother us. She had sealed her fate with Pixie, Rosebud, Hero and Tinkerbell, and we were going to take her down. The only questions that remained were when and how.

Martha met Aji and tried to bond with her. Daddy had explained to us that it might be difficult for Aji to look after us as she got older, and we knew we were a handful, so we gave it a chance. We would do anything for Aji and were willing to put up with Martha if Aji liked her. But when Martha met Aji, she told her that as a school teacher, she would soon teach us how to behave.

That statement made Aji's eyes flash. We might have been rowdy and noisy and she loudly condemned our behaviour every day, but to Aji, staunchly defensive of her son and her grandchildren, this was blasphemy. She decided to tolerate Martha for our sakes, so that maybe she could teach us a bit about the Bible, which was after all, half of our heritage.

Daddy never liked Martha's mincing ways, but he hoped we would benefit from her school teacher background. And so, with the noblest of intentions, all of us decided to put up with Martha for the sake of each other.

But Martha soon began to dig a deep hole for herself. She laid out pretty frocks and collared shirts for us to put on after school, and refused to let us wear our old shorts and soft hand-me-down tees.

We smiled heroically and put up with her.

She tried to make Kuku and Ritu wear ribbons in their hair. Daddy and Aji were cautiously pleased but extremely doubtful when she sewed us matching bows from pink striped cloth: hairbands with bows for the girls and a neat bowtie for a glowering Hero.

And still we put up with her.

On Sundays, she asked Daddy to take her to the local church for mass, which Daddy did without fail. We liked to wake up early on Sundays and make mud pies, but Martha said we were being ungodly and forced us to go with her. She made us put on our itchiest clothes and sit in church while the best and sunniest hours of the morning ticked by.

And still we put up with her.

She stood over us at the dinner table and tried to steer our conversation into a more productive direction. We liked to play Catch the Rat in the Trap at dinner. We had made this game up recently and it always sent us into gales of laughter.

Kuku started. "Let's play Catch the Rat in the Trap".

I replied. "No, I'm bored of that game. Let's play Catch the Rat in the Trap instead."

Izzy slammed his fist onto the table. "No! I never win that game. I'm only playing with you if you play Catch the Rat in the Trap."

Ritu turned her nose up. "Come on, Izzy. We play that every day. Let's play something else. I know! Let's play Catch the Rat in the Trap."

I replied. "You always want to play your games, Ritu. We're playing Catch the Rat in the Trap."

We could go for hours, replying faster and faster and stopping only when we were breathless with giggles. The first time they heard it, Pinky and Mahua understood within seconds, and always dived into the game enthusiastically.

But Martha followed the lines with difficulty, hoping that we would actually get to the game at some point, trying to make sense of something that made no sense. When she couldn't take it any longer, she ordered us to stop and discuss what we were grateful for instead.

And still we put up with her.

Then one day, she asked Tulsi Bai not to cook because she was going to make us eat boiled vegetables. Every day of our childhood, Tulsi Bai made her delicious *varan* for us and we ate it with rice or with different *sabzis*. Even when there was *biriyani* made at home, we had to have our *varan* on the side.

Usually we ate our vegetables without a fuss, although we liked them best when they were fresh and crunchy. But Martha had boiled all the colour out of the vegetables and slopped them onto the plates in front of us, and we couldn't bring ourselves to taste it.

Izzy looked at his grey boiled cabbage doubtfully. "Can I put some *varan* on it?"

"No. You can't eat *varan* with everything. You have to develop a palate for different types of food."

"But this is yucky."

"It's not yucky; it's good for you. It'll make you strong."

Kuku leapt to his defence. "He can swing up to the first branch of the mango tree with just his fingertips, you know."

Martha ignored this and turned to Ritu, who had picked up a limp bean on her fork and was slowly sticking her tongue out to touch it. "Come on, Rosebud. I'm sure you'll like it."

"It smells like cardboard" said Ritu baldly.

Martha turned to me. I was trying to be a grown-up and eat a piece of carrot, but it was as unappealing as rubber. I could see Tulsi Bai hovering in the doorway, hands on her hips, waiting to be called on to hand out *varan* and *chapatis*. "Tulsi Bai makes us baked vegetables with white sauce. Can we do that instead?"

"No, that's only cheese and salt and flour. You have to learn what all vegetables taste like…"

But Martha was interrupted by horrible retching sounds. Kuku sat there, her chin barely at the level of the table and vomited straight into her plate. A piece of boiled mushroom came out and Kuku's eyes welled up. The three of us knew that Kuku could make herself vomit at will (it was one of her greatest talents) so we weren't overly concerned. But Martha panicked.

"Oh Pixie, didn't you chew it properly?" Martha cried, hurrying over to dab Kuku's chin with a table napkin.

Kuku jerked her head away, swiped at her chin with the back of her hand, and glared up at Martha. "This is disgusting. I'm not going to eat any more." And with that, she slid off her chair and walked into Tulsi Bai's welcoming arms.

Encouraged by this, we left the dining table too and told Martha we would feed the boiled vegetables to Mr. Waffles and his babies, IF they wanted it. Martha disappeared into her bedroom in a huff, and the four of us ate big plates of *varan* and rice without her annoying presence hovering over our dinner.

That night, we lay in bed and decided we'd had enough of Martha. We laid our plans in fierce whispers in the dark. We could sense that Tulsi Bai didn't like her, and we were quite sure that Daddy and Aji were annoyed by her too, but none of the grown-ups would ever admit it. It was up to us.

From the next day, our campaign began. It was not for nothing that we had watched *Dennis the Menace* and *Problem Child* many times over. We put earthworms and all kinds of bugs in her bed. We poured water into her shoes. We threw her hairbrush onto the roof so she couldn't find it.

And then one Saturday morning, when Kuku and Ritu were floating about looking for the cat, they wandered over to Martha's side of the house and discovered that she was sitting on the potty with the bathroom door ajar. It was time for Kuku and Ritu, Pixie and

Rosebud, to execute the *piece de resistance*. There was no time to consult the wiser elders of the gang, so instead they planned their own stunt.

Kuku stuck her head around the door and crowed "Cock a doodle dooooo...", and then disappeared.

Then Ritu stuck her head around the door and crowed "Beat you black and bluuuuue...", before disappearing.

Both of them stuck their heads around the door, sang out "Cock a doodle dooooo" and dissolved into giggles before scampering off.

It wasn't as creative or wicked as Izzy and I would have wanted, but it worked.

Daddy was reading the papers peacefully and drinking his first cup of tea with Aji, when Martha came storming out of her room. "Nitin, this is the absolute limit, I must say! You have to discipline these children."

Aji's eyes narrowed as she looked at us. Kuku and Ritu were sitting with their colouring books, plying the crayons industriously. They looked exceedingly angelic, which was always a bad sign.

Daddy put down his newspapers in consternation. "What? What did they do now? Bugs in your bed?"

Izzy and I were eating our morning *chapati* and jam nearby, and we heard the conversation. We sensed that an almighty fuss was about to take place and wandered out to witness it.

Martha was trembling with rage and embarrassment. "No! They sang a song to me while I was .... umm...in the bathroom."

"They sang a song?" Daddy was bewildered. "What? Were they hiding in the bathroom? How..."

Martha started to cry. "The door was open, and they said that they'll beat me black and blue."

Daddy was shocked. He rounded on us. "What? Who did that?"

"It's that song, Daddy. From *Lady and the Tramp*." Kuku used her softest voice and widest eyes. "We just sang it for Aunty Martha. Cock a doodle do. Beat you….."

Here Kuku's voice hiccupped and faded, but Ritu piped in to encourage her. "Beat you black and blue…"

Daddy looked from Kuku to Martha, and the faintest shadow of amusement began to appear in his eyes. It was the last straw for Martha. She began crying, pouring her woes out to Daddy, who tried to pacify her, but she refused to listen.

"Nitin, I've tried my best but these children…" She shuddered and then straightened up piously. "They're just ungodly!"

Izzy gave me a sidelong grin and Martha happened to catch it. She flew into a temper and screamed that she wouldn't stay in this madhouse any longer.

Aji pinched her lips together and herded us into the other room so the grown-ups could talk. We dug our heels into the floor and stiffened our legs, wanting to hear what Martha said, but Aji pushed us into the bedroom impatiently and told us to be quiet for a while.

The next day, Martha was put onto the bus back to Goa. While Daddy went to the counter to pay for the ticket, we waved to Martha politely as she sat in the window seat. She sniffed and pointedly turned her face away. It was a good thing that she wasn't looking, because we shrugged and sniggered. To emphasise our feelings, Izzy cupped his hands around his mouth and made a rude farting sound.

When we got home, Hero took his striped bowtie out of his desk and jumped up and down on it. We watched solemnly until it was destroyed, and with that brief ceremony, the four of us returned to our ungodly ways.

CHAPTER NINE

Whirlpool Weekend

When Kuku and Ritu were toddlers, they had velvety brown eyes and soft silky hair with the fringe cut straight across their foreheads. They were barely a year apart and were like twins in many ways. They completed each other's sentences, cried when the other cried, laughed when the other laughed, and could keep each other entertained for hours.

Ritu had pale milky skin but her freckles came in later, just like a Dalmatian puppy. She was reserved when she met new people, but those that she loved, she loved fiercely. She had skinny arms and legs and looked fragile, but as we knew, she could also be pure evil.

Kuku was the opposite. She was a strong baby who loved everyone and laughed a lot. She had sturdy brown limbs and rough round cheeks that we all loved to stroke. She had a smile that could light up the room, and was happy to waddle behind us and be pushed around as long as she was included in all our games.

Many years later, Mahua's mother told me about a terrible game she once caught us playing during a dinner party one night. The grown-ups were in the garden and the kids were supposed to be eating at the table. But instead we had propped up a chubby 2-year old Kuku on a chair, and instructed her to cling with all her might to the backrest. Ritu, Izzy and I stood beside her and shook the chair, doing all we could to knock her off.

By the time we were discovered, she had already been rolled onto the floor a couple of times but she was beaming with excitement at being allowed to play with us.

One hot Sunday morning, Kuku (now 6 years, still chubby) was delighted to be at the centre of attention again. It was Pool Day and we were sitting around Aji, eating hot *chapatis* with *ghee* and sugar. Kuku's milk tooth had been growing looser every day, and it felt like today was the day it would fall out. She showed it to Aji and wiggled it with her tongue.

"Looks like you'll be putting it under your pillow tonight, Kuku" Aji said, distracting her so she could feed her the last few bites of *chapati*.

"I'm going to catch the ..." Kuku mumbled around her mouthful.

"What's that? What did you say?"

Kuku swallowed the last morsel and stood up. "I'm going to catch the Tooth Fairy tonight. And I'm going to put her in a jar and make her my pet."

Aji was shocked. Her precious little golden grandchild had a black heart. "But babloo, the Tooth Fairy is a good person. She flies around the world, collecting all the teeth that little children lose, and giving them a coin in exchange for it."

"I don't care. I want to catch her. I want her to take me to the Tooth Castle."

The Tooth Castle is the giant castle that the Tooth Fairy builds with all the teeth she gets from us kids. That's why she pays for it. We all knew that, but only Kuku had the burning desire and the gumption to devise a plan like this.

That morning, the three of us knew that Kuku had come into her own. She would be fit to play with, not because Aji said "let her tag along, poor thing", but because she had earned our respect with a scheme like this. As we changed into our swimming costumes, we developed and discarded a dozen plans to catch the elusive Tooth Fairy.

We always looked forward to Pool Day. There was a small round pond in the front of our house that was about 15 feet wide and only 4 feet deep. Daddy didn't fill it up all the way to the top because he was worried we'd drown each other in it. But on the rare occasions when it was almost full, it meant we could make a whirlpool.

Our whirlpools were things of beauty, our very own science experiment. We needed at least six kids for this, so we only did it when we had friends over. If we waded in the same direction for long enough, the water started swirling in a fast-moving whirlpool. We were still waiting to see if it could actually suck someone under, with Pinky volunteering to jump in because she was the thinnest and lightest. We'd tried this a few times but hadn't had any luck so far.

Zayra and Aaliya were dropped off, traces of milk moustaches from their hurried breakfast still showing and we explained how we wanted to capture the Tooth Fairy. Even though they didn't believe in any of this, the Tooth Fairy campaign was too exciting to remain sceptical about, and soon they were hatching devious plans with us. Pinky arrived and was pulled straight out of her father's jeep and into the midst of our scheming.

We clambered into the pool and stood in the water while we argued about the best way to trap the Tooth Fairy. Kuku, Pinky and

Aaliya were considerably shorter than all of us and had to bounce on tiptoes to keep their chins above water, but eventually they were the ones who came up with the winning plan.

When the tooth fell out, we'd tie a thin thread around it and put it under the pillow. All of us would pretend to be asleep, and when the Tooth Fairy arrived, Kuku would tug on the thread to lure the Tooth Fairy in under the pillow. We'd capture her there and slip her into a jar. After that, we could take her to school and make the

other kids pay money to see her. We could even train her to give us Tooth Money without waiting for our teeth to fall out.

Once the planning was done, it was time to get down to business. We had a whirlpool to make and it would soon be snack time.

"Let's start now, quickly" ordered Izzy. For some reason, it was always Izzy who orchestrated the whirlpool. "Kuku, Pinky, stop fooling about with the fungus! Start walking."

We moved to the edges of the round pool, turned to our left, and began walking in the chin-deep water as fast as we could. Nobody could stop for any reason and if you wanted to pee, you had to do it in the water while you walked. If the person behind you felt a sudden warm current in the water, so be it. It would wash off anyway.

"Put your arms out. Go faster" Izzy screamed. We leaned forward and spread our arms out to push more water. The water started to swirl in a slow circle.

"Don't stop to look at it! We'll stop later. Keep going. Keep going!" All of us responded to the urgency in his voice and began to take bigger steps in the water. As the momentum of the water became stronger, it started to push us till we were almost running.

A few minutes later, we had a definite whirlpool going. The water eddied around so fast that it was strong enough to move us if we stopped running. It was time to test the power of the whirlpool. Izzy and I grabbed Pinky and pushed her up onto the edge of the pool.

She lay there panting for a few seconds and then stood up. She looked like a small wet mouse, with her high ponytail askew and her thin shoulders shivering. "Izzy, Izzy! I think I might go under this time" she cried.

"Maybe, if we're lucky. We're all here, don't worry. We'll pull you out. Now, when I say *Three*, you jump into the middle of the whirlpool, okay?"

Pinky knew her role, but she nodded and stood up straight.

All of us crouched and took up fielding positions like we'd seen in cricket matches, even though we were bobbing in a circle. Izzy eyed the whirlpool and looked around to check that there were no grown-ups watching. Pinky was ready. The water was seething and swirling. It was time.

He raised his hand like the good showman he was, and we held our breath.

"One! Two! Thr…"

Splaaashhhhhh! Pinky couldn't contain her excitement. All we saw was a glimpse of her scrawny brown legs flailing as she flew through the air and landed straight in the centre of the whirlpool. Her tiny frame was tossed around for half a second and then she disappeared into the water.

We peered at the water, bobbing silently and feeling a bit of concern for the first time. Daddy had been telling us for a long time not to leap into the shallow pool, but we never really paid much attention to that. I was the eldest one here, and if anything happened….

Pinky burst out of the water, spitting and pushing her collapsed ponytail out of the way. She was so stunned by the jump that she couldn't hold herself steady in the swirling water. We cheered and laughed – she may not have been truly sucked under, but it was always fun to watch her being tossed around like a small shrimp.

Later that morning, Kanappa brought us fresh watermelon sliced up by Tulsi Bai and we paused our games to dig in. Izzy and I sat together, spitting seeds into the pool, while the smallies worked on their underwater breathing skills, diving under to retrieve the seeds.

"Mahi, what happens to the rest of the world if we kidnap the Tooth Fairy?" Izzy had droplets of water on his eyelashes, and his spiky hair was plastered to his head like a shiny helmet. He looked like a baby seal.

"I'm sure there are lots of Tooth Fairies. Imagine how many teeth they have to collect every night. Every kid who loses a tooth puts it under the pillow. And then if there's only one Tooth Fairy, how does she build the castle? She needs lots of fairies."

Izzy thought about this carefully. "But what if she's the main one? The rest of them won't know what to do if she's gone."

"They might come to rescue her," I said idly, picking at the scab on my knee. His sharp intake of breath made me look up.

"Do you think they'll all come here to take her back?" His eyes were alight at the thought.

For a moment we were distracted by visions of an epic battle between us and the fairies, but then Kuku's tooth fell out and we turned to planning the great capture.

That evening, when Pinky's dad came by to pick her up, she threw a tantrum and refused to go. It was her signature move and we had seen it many times, but we always stopped to watch in awe. For such a puny creature, no taller than 3 feet, she could make grown-ups crumble within minutes. She was convinced that the capture of the Tooth Fairy would be the most magical event in her life, and nobody, not even her father, would be able to tear her away.

Pinky's dad made some mild protests, but when he glanced apologetically at Aji, she gestured to him that Pinky could stay. There was always room for our best friends at home, and diminutive Pinky had won her heart too. And so Pinky got to stay for the night.

When Pinky stayed over, she shared Kuku's pillow and blanket and squeezed in next to me. They giggled together under their breath until they fell asleep, or they whined until I put my book down and told them a story. Ritu tucked herself into her lower bunk with at least one cat under the blanket, and Izzy retired to his top bunk, settling in with a reminder that he was most likely to catch the Tooth Fairy because he was higher up.

As usual, a few minutes later, I heard Kuku's voice in the dark. "Mahi, tell us a story."

I thought for a minute and asked them what they wanted to hear about: the grey kitten who cut its claws, or Mala, the girl with one brown eye and one green eye. They always chose Mala. Over a year ago, I'd made up a story about a girl called Mala. Kuku and Ritu liked her so much that I had to make up regular stories about Mala's life.

It became like one of those serials on TV that Aji watched. Pinky asked for updates on Mala in school every day, so she knew all the latest events in this fictional character's life.

I sighed and began. "One day, Mala and her friends decided to make a whirlpool in their pool…."

Izzy, far away from us in his bunk bed, was the first one to drop off. We heard his gentle snores soon. Ritu drifted off next, drowsy and warm with a soft purring cat under her chin. Kuku and Pinky were still vibrating with adrenaline, so they remained wide awake for a long time. They weren't shy of prodding me awake when my voice tapered off. I told the story for longer than I realised, talking long after my mind had fallen asleep.

The next morning, we woke up to a big disappointment. Kuku and Pinky sat in Aji's lap, crying bitterly as they explained how they fell asleep and missed the Tooth Fairy. The sole coin that was left in exchange for Kuku's tooth was no consolation, but Aji patted them and fed them jam and *chapatis*, and promised them they only had to wait until the next tooth fell out.

CHAPTER TEN

Izzy's All-You-Can-Eat Guppy Buffet

As Izzy approached his tenth birthday, he developed a sudden and intense fascination with fish. Nobody remembers how it came about, but he began to doodle fish in his notebooks and ask for a fish tank. He kept up a constant whine for a couple of months and out of solidarity we added to it, until finally Izzy was allowed to get a bowl with a goldfish.

From the bowl, he progressed very quickly to a small square tank. It surprised all of us to see our kick-boxing, jump-kicking, sucker-punching brother use the gentlest of hands to transfer his solo fish and clean the tank. With Izzy's birthday coming up fast, Daddy decided to rope in Kanappa and make a giant fish tank for a birthday present.

They began a top-secret project in the outhouse, sneaking in long sheets of toughened glass when Izzy wasn't around. I was the only one let in on the secret because they needed an assistant to ferry cups of tea and hold sheets of glass at exactly the right angle.

Daddy used a silicone gun and glued the sheets together, while Kanappa and I supported the heavy glass until our arms ached. We polished and adjusted the tank all day, and when we finally stepped back, we had made a 6 foot long, 2 foot high fish tank that would take

Izzy's breath away. We sipped our tea while the silicone joints dried, and then filled it painstakingly, one bucket at a time to test its strength.

At dinner time that night, as we milled about around Tulsi Bai waiting to be served, we heard a loud CRAACCKKK, just like a gunshot, coming from the outhouse. It sounded like firecrackers to everyone else, but Daddy and I knew what it was. He leapt up from his chair in alarm and then, catching sight of Izzy's enquiring face, sank back with an anguished look.

The glass tank must have shattered, splashing litres of water all over the room and ruining hours of hard work. Daddy buried himself grumpily behind his newspaper, his mind working furiously on the problem.

When we got new sheets of glass the next day, Daddy used silicone gel lavishly and added metal elbow joints on the corners to give it extra strength. We filled it up again, and this time, Kanappa added ropes around it to hold it together while the gel hardened.

And it worked. On Izzy's birthday, we wheeled it into position in the verandah, and took him to see his new fish tank. We stood back, pleased to see his eyes growing as round as saucers. Over the next few hours, he poured in the pebbles from his smaller tank and lovingly transferred his single goldfish into it.

The goldfish was no bigger than his thumb, and it looked woefully tiny in the 6-foot long tank, finning energetically to get all the way to the other side. Even with the addition of an extra bag of pebbles, the tank appeared vast and empty.

Thus began Izzy's yearlong campaign of wheedling Aji into giving him extra coins and extorting money from us. As soon as he'd saved up enough, Izzy would cycle off, his short legs pumping furiously, to pay a visit to Ronny the Crook.

Ronny had earned his moniker by selling fish that would die a few short days after you brought them home. His house was lined with fish tanks illuminated in shades of electric blue and neon pink. He always had rock ballads pulsing from speakers because he claimed it soothed the fish. Ronny procured top quality rare fish for serious fish enthusiasts, but small snotty-nosed boys like Izzy were easily parted from their money, and eagerly took home the most damaged specimens.

Every time Izzy went off to meet Ronny the Crook, we waited to see what he came back with, and it was always something rare and beautiful, with just *one thing* wrong with it. A vibrant Clownfish with bright orange fins and a big growth on its head. A glorious black and white Angel Fish with a waving dorsal fin and a semi-healed scar where the bottom fin should have been. A Neon Tetra with a permanent diarrhoea problem.

Our garden is filled with tiny tombstones of the dozens of fish we buried in those initial months, until Daddy realised it was happening a little too frequently and made some enquiries. He found someone else who also sold fish, albeit without the electrifying rock music soundtrack in the background, and took Izzy there to learn about fish.

Once Izzy transferred his patronage from Ronny the Crook and adopted a more measured approach, the tank began to look truly beautiful. Izzy saved up for a water filter, installed wooden logs and swaying aquarium plants to create an underwater landscape, and learned how to clean his tank. He started off with guppies, tiny iridescent fish with showy fins and tails that were perfect for a beginner. The tank was soon filled with over 30 healthy guppies in blue, green, pink, and orange.

Izzy and I were put on tank-cleaning duty and spent Saturday afternoons moving the fish into a bucket, keeping the murderous cats at a safe distance, and changing the water. Siphoning the dirty water out involved some science, which Izzy assured me he had mastered.

We put a long pipe into the tank and sucked at the outlet end a few times to create a vacuum. As the suction pulled the water out, it cleaned out any debris from the tank as well. But in our enthusiasm, we usually sucked too hard and didn't take our heads away in time, and so over the years, Izzy and I swallowed litres of water filled with fish potty.

With time, Izzy's understanding of fish grew. He began to read books about aquarium care so we deferred to his greater knowledge and allowed him to tell us what to do.

One day Kuku and Ritu went running to him to tell him that one of the guppies was swimming belly-up along the bottom of the tank. Izzy eyed it for some time doubtfully and then pronounced his diagnosis: that it was merely scratching its back. We accepted this and went back to our games, but the next morning, the fish was dead.

Izzy performed the funeral on his own so he could say sorry to it, and began to read more intensively, until he could quote passages and descriptions to us.

The guppies suffered a major setback when Izzy brought home two real-life piranhas. He had wanted them for months and had finally located a pair. He told us that if you dipped your finger into the water, the piranhas would attack and eat it, bone and all, till only a stub was left. With great meaning in his eyes, he picked up Kuku's chubby forearm and acted like he was weighing it, sending her crying to Aji while he cackled and ran off.

When the piranhas actually arrived, we were disappointed by their insignificant appearance. They were ugly creatures with dead eyes, moving sluggishly in the plastic bag that Izzy held aloft. We were sure they couldn't be the flesh-eating zombie fish that we'd seen in the movies and mocked Izzy for being cheated yet again.

Izzy's face fell and eager to console him, we told him we should keep them anyway, just in case they grew into fearsome killers when they were bigger. Izzy cheered up immediately and stood on a stool to slide the piranhas gently into the tank with his long-handled net. We shrugged and stood around to watch the new fish settle in.

It happened so fast that we were all paralysed. In a few seconds, the piranhas were zooming through the tank, systematically polishing off every guppy that crossed their path. They must have wolfed down at least ten guppies each, and all chaos broke loose.

Izzy almost dived into the tank to stop them, and after much running about and bumping into each other, we finally managed to catch the piranhas in a net and plop them into a bucket.

The guppy population, now tragically halved, managed to survive the onslaught and prosper over the years. We often stood beside the tank, tapping at the glass and enjoying these active, curious creatures who swam closer to greet us. Although we hated the piranhas from that day on, we had developed a strange kind of respect for them and decided that we had to keep them.

Decades later, those piranhas still live in the small tank that we keep in a corner, with their dead eyes staring out at us, living off scraps of meat and dreaming of the day they gorged at Izzy's All-You-Can-Eat Guppy Buffet.

CHAPTER ELEVEN

Finger-Flavoured Ice-Cream

As the last of the monsoon clouds departed from Belgaum skies, the weather began to grow warmer. We had one month of October heat before the winter chill truly set in, and it usually coincided with the Diwali holidays.

For the four of us, having completed weeks of feverish studying for our mid-term exams, the start of our month-long holiday was a time for celebration. We shoved our books into our desks, pushed our uniforms to the back of the cupboard, and prepared ourselves for a few glorious weeks with no school and no homework.

We spent mornings turning cardboard boxes into ships that sailed in crocodile-infested waters, practising cartwheels in the pool, or chasing each other at breakneck speed on cycles through the Fort. When we were summoned indoors in the afternoon to avoid the hottest hours of the day, we retired to the cool, quiet living room and sprawled out on the carpet under the fan.

This year, we had a new batch of baby rabbits from Mr. Waffles' grandchildren, so we locked all the doors to keep Eclipse out and brought the little bunny babies in to be with us. For two hours, the house was blissfully quiet as we coloured in our books, read about the adventures of the *Famous Five*, or dozed with the rabbits around us.

Daddy, incurably active at the best of times, was tiresomely creative when it came to developing new projects for us to help with. He recruited us to clean and sort our book collections, drain and scrub the pool, or paint the planetary system on the walls of our spare room.

One morning, we were helping Daddy and Kanappa to empty the spare rooms in the outhouse, which functioned as storerooms for us. Rum and Raisin, who were not allowed to enter our house, were delighted to be let into these rooms with us. They romped about under our feet, bringing bits of rubbish in their mouths every few minutes.

Izzy spotted something that looked interesting and pushed the dogs aside with a cry, diving into a pile of old boxes. We waited patiently for him to emerge and saw that he'd unearthed a large wooden bucket with a metal contraption attached to it.

The four of us gathered around it eagerly. When Daddy came up to see what on earth was taking us so long to find the broom, he found us arguing about what it was. When he explained to us that it was an ice-cream maker, it sent us into a tizzy of excitement.

Naturally we began to plan an ice-cream party, the likes of which had never been seen before. We would serve mountains of fresh ice-cream that had been made right in front of us, in a rainbow of flavours and colours.

It took two days of planning and the combined efforts of the whole household to prepare for this party. Aji and Tulsi Bai ordered extra packets of milk, boiled and cooled the many litres, and then made place in our fridge to store the vessels. Kanappa was sent off to the market to buy ice and flavours, while we painstakingly chopped up fruit and nuts to sprinkle on top.

On the day of the party, all our friends turned up with expectant faces. Daddy dusted off the wooden ice-cream churner and sat on the steps with the bucket gripped between his knees. Kanappa poured the milk into the steel canister in the middle and hammered the ice into chunks so he could fit it into the bucket. Then we stood around Daddy, breathing down his neck while he jiggled the stiff handle and began to turn it.

An hour later, we were all disappointed and Daddy was getting cranky. Kanappa and he were taking turns to churn the ice-cream, rubbing their aching arms and shoulders while batting us away. But when they pulled out the small canister of ice-cream to serve it, everyone got only one small scoop. There were too many of us and the canister was too small.

Daddy looked at us milling around, dejected and beginning to squabble and kick each other, and he tossed the bucket aside. "Right! Come on everyone, hop into the Sumo! We're going to Kaveri. It'll take all afternoon to do this."

We've never moved so fast before. Within minutes, the four of us, with Pinky, Zayra, Aaliya, Mahua, and a few others who had shown up, stuffed ourselves like sardines into the back of the Sumo, while Daddy and Kanappa jumped into the front seat.

Kaveri Cold Drink House was a two-storied restaurant that stood right in the middle of the bustling market. It had a well-loved air to it, with battered velvet seats and ornate wooden tables that were criss-crossed with scratches. A murky fish tank guarded the entry, photographs of fruit custards and triple-layered sundaes dotted the walls, and fans whirred softly inside. Even on the sunniest day, the interior of Kaveri was dim and cool, and the air was fragrant with mango and butterscotch and chocolate.

We entered Kaveri with our senses tingling, already able to taste our favourite flavours on our tongues. Waiters hurried about with loaded trays of ice-cream cups balanced above their heads, swerving to avoid the toddlers who played between tables.

Daddy stopped to chat with the owner, but we raced up the stairs two at a time, heading to the 'Family Section' where the tables were bigger and small booths with curtains offered privacy.

A pair of lovers were feeding each other ice-cream and sharing a bottle of Maaza, but we interrupted their idyll with loud shrieks. They looked up in alarm as we swarmed past to get to the best seat by the window. A heavy cloud of aftershave emanated from the boy, who shot daggers from his eyes at our rude intrusion.

But we were between the ages of 6-11 and had finished our exams just a few days ago. We were impervious to any daggers and had only enough room for one thought in our head: What flavour were we going to order? The mango ice-cream was always good but it didn't have crunchy bits in it like the butterscotch. The cassata offered three flavours in one but then did we want to miss out on the specialty flavour, Fruit 'n' Nut? And did we want to get the exciting alien-green *vala* drink or the *pachak* that fizzed into our noses and made our burps taste of ginger all day?

The Family Section was presided over by the oldest waiter in Kaveri. We called him the Gold Miner because he always stood on the side of the room picking his nose. After a deep exploration of his nostrils, he'd examine his finger intently, roll his fingers together to make a ball of 'the gold', and then flick it onto the floor. The first time we were here, Izzy watched this ritual carefully and picked up every mannerism, imitating him so well at home that Daddy had to threaten him with all kinds of punishment to make him stop.

The Gold Miner also walked with a limp and had a white cataract over one eye, and in any other setting, we would have run from him, screaming for our lives. But in Kaveri, he was the one who brought our ice-cream so we hailed him like an old friend. Only seven-year old Ritu seemed to be scared of him. She often walked in a wide circle around him and jumped when he appeared beside our table in the dimly lit parlour.

The tables in the ice-cream parlour were ostensibly four-seaters, but the tables were narrow and offered no leg-room. We usually went as a group, with our friends and outhouse kids tagging along, so the waiters pushed tables together in a long row against a wall so that we could sit together.

All the kids jammed themselves in, and Daddy and any other grown-ups who had come with us sat at one end of the row, perched uncomfortably at the small table with their legs sticking out across the aisle. This arrangement meant they were too far from us to tell us what to do.

Free from any laws, our visits to the ice-cream parlour were subject to the rules of the jungle, which said that only the fittest and fastest would survive. We kicked each other under the table and shoved each other's elbows off the table to make place for our own. If the youngest or weakest members didn't eat quickly, the bigger kids dipped their spoons in or just snatched the cups. After Pinky showed us how to drink a soft drink so fast that it fizzed out of your nose, our visits also ended with at least one kid choking or everyone's clothes covered in sticky green vala.

The Gold Miner took our order unsmilingly, without bothering to write it down, and returned with his own interpretation of the flavours we wanted. By the time he creaked up and down the stairs and brought us our goodies, we had usually forgotten our orders, so we ate whatever he put in front of us. But this time, Ritu decided she wanted vanilla.

When the Gold Miner handed her a cone of Tutti Frutti ice-cream, she lifted her chin rebelliously and declared that she didn't want it. The old man opened his single eye wide and pushed the cone closer to her, but she folded her arms and sat back.

"No! I wanted vanilla. I don't want Tutti Frutti."

"But it is vanilla ice-cream. We just put a topping of Tutti Frutti on it."

"But I don't want any topping. I only want vanilla."

All of us looked from Ritu to the waiter. If he went back to get her a vanilla cone, one of us would get the Tutti Frutti. We leaned forward imperceptibly, spooning up our ice-creams quickly because Daddy would hand it to the one who had finished their own share.

The waiter looked sourly at Ritu's small, pale face and then back at the stairs. It was a long way to go for one cone, on a bad leg. Then the solution dawned on him and a smile cracked the wrinkled surface of his face.

"If you don't want the Tutti Frutti," he said, pinching his thumb and forefinger together and flicking each Tutti Frutti piece off the top of the ice-cream, "no problem. Let's throw them all away."

We watched as the Gold Miner's grimy fingernails swiped at her ice-cream, knocking off the topping she didn't want. Pieces of Tutti Frutti landed on our table and flew off into the dim depths of the Family Section. Izzy dodged a flying piece and giggled with delight. When the waiter was done, he held the cone out to Ritu again, this time with no Tutti Frutti.

Mahua and I, stuck on the other side of the table, shivered at the sight of the tracks left in the ice-cream by his disgusting fingers. We knew Ritu would kick up a fuss. She was as fastidious about her food as her precious cats were, and almost snarled if you tried to share food off her plate. But instead, we watched in horror as she received the cone, gulped, screwed up her face and took a big lick.

The Gold Miner stood there until she had eaten half the scoop and then stumped off, mumbling to himself. It was too late to stop Ritu, and once she had started, it would have been a shame to waste the ice-cream. We watched in awe as she soldiered on, only tearing our eyes away from her when our own scoops began to melt.

Ritu was only seven years old when this happened, but the jokes about her favourite Finger Flavoured ice-cream followed her for years after.

CHAPTER TWELVE

Belly Flops and Nose Dives

As much as we longed for the life of the Famous Five, who seemed to have no adult supervision at all, we were very accustomed to Daddy planning our days and deciding what we would do on our weekends. We just didn't know it yet.

Just before our mid-term exams, as we frantically mugged up reams of text books, we had received an extraordinary piece of good news. Daddy was going to be travelling to China as a consultant for a television programme and would be gone for at least three weeks.

This meant that once we finished our exams, we would have three weeks with no school and no Daddy to keep an eye on us. Aji was too tender-hearted to truly discipline us, and we knew we could easily wrap her around our little fingers. We just knew it was going to be the best October we'd ever had.

A week after the holidays arrived, shortly after our ice-cream party and the Finger Flavour disaster, Daddy departed for China. We promised to be good, waved him off at the gate, and then came back into the house, wondering what we would do with our new freedom.

We spent the first two days climbing trees and cycling around the Fort, but we couldn't think of anything significant to mark our new freedom. Aji began to notice that we were acting aimless.

Without Daddy striding around the house and telling us what to do, without the risk of a quick cuff on the ear or the terrifying 'big eyes' warning look, it felt like something was missing. When Daddy wasn't around, we didn't have anyone to show off to when we reached the top branches of the mango tree, or to run up to with the new joke we had just made up.

If you had told us that we were missing Daddy, we wouldn't have believed it. We wanted to be independent and allowed to do exactly what we wanted. But for the four of us, between the ages of 6 to 11 years, Daddy stood at the centre of our universe and without his presence, we felt adrift. And therefore, as was to be expected, we started acting up.

We decided that Eclipse had fishy breath and tried to brush his teeth with toothpaste, causing him to snarl and scratch Izzy on the cheek. Kuku and Ritu took to walking along the flower beds, whipping the marigold heads off the stems, pretending to be teachers disciplining bad students. Kanappa allowed us to get away with almost anything, but if we dared to pluck a single flower in the garden, it made him hop with rage.

Of all the grannies we knew in Belgaum, Aji was the most laid-back. She seemed to truly enjoy our company, and even our friends always got a hug and a snack from her. Whether we were roaring past in the midst of a heated battle, tumbling around her playing violent games, or crawling under her chair to grab the kittens or puppies who hid under her sari, she didn't bat an eyelid. But she too had limits to her leniency. Disrespecting Kanappa, Tulsi Bai or anyone who worked in our home was strictly not allowed.

So she took it seriously when Izzy overstepped his limits that week. He was moseying through the garden, his pockets filled with sugary *boondi*, mulling over what to do next. Every now and then, he drew out a fistful of *boondi*, plucked out the loose threads and lint from his pocket, and shoved it into his mouth. He happened to spot Kanappa weeding the flower beds, squatting on the ground under a coconut tree.

Izzy scurried behind a bush, took aim, and began to pelt *boondi* at Kanappa's head.

A few minutes later, he was frogmarched into the house, crying indignantly because Kanappa had threatened to smack him. Aji gave Izzy a scolding he wouldn't forget – it cut deep because she never really shouted at us – and so all of us decided to behave for the afternoon.

By the next day, we had recovered from our chastised mood and were planning our daily wrestling match, inspired by the World Wrestling Federation. The four of us stood at each corner of the carpet and Izzy counted down like they did on television. At his signal, we leapt into the middle of the carpet and pounded anyone whom our fists landed on.

The wrestling usually escalated if someone took offence to an injury, leading to an all-out fight, and Tulsi Bai and Aji would have to wade in and pull us apart. One or two of us usually emerged from this with bloody scratches and purple bruises, which was another of Aji's strict no-nos.

That day, after pulling Kuku out of the tangle of limbs and discovering her precious pet had sustained a nosebleed, Aji was at her wit's end. By now, we had almost killed the cat, we had ruined the garden, we had upset Kanappa, and there was no doubt that we would soon probably kill each other.

A lucky call from a friend revealed that another family in the Fort had signed up Andy, their equally rambunctious son, for swimming classes. Andy's grateful mother assured Aji that the early morning timing combined with vigorous physical activity would tire us out and keep us out of trouble for the rest of the day. By the time the holidays were over, we would have learned a new skill and Aji would have been able to enjoy her morning tea in peace.

We were promptly signed up for the classes and Andy's dad, Uncle Srikanth agreed to pick us up and drop us off every morning. There was a swimming aptitude test the next day, he said, and we could join the new batch immediately after that.

On the first day we went, we joined dozens of other kids who were standing in line, waiting for their turn. The swimming instructor called the first kid up, gripped them under the shoulders and took them out into deep water. There, after warning them to hold their breath, they dipped him or her under the water and brought them up a few seconds later. If the kid choked or cried, it meant they had failed the test and couldn't join swimming classes that year. If they managed to stay alive and smile, they could join the classes.

All the parents accepted this scientific test of their child's aptitude, and stood beside the line, giving their kids quiet instructions on how to pass the test.

I went in. A short, fat instructor in a swimming cap took me in, shouted some instructions, dipped me under, and I emerged without any trouble. Izzy came up beaming. Both of us passed the test and went to stand on one side of the pool with the winners.

When Ritu's turn came, she squirmed and thrashed and ignored all instructions. He shouted instructions before dipping her, but she hadn't taken a breath and emerged from the water like an angry wet cat, scowling and spitting. He tried to say something comforting to her but when Ritu kneed him in the crotch, he swore in Kannada and tossed her into the shallow end for the parents to fish out.

Kuku went in smoothly, followed all the instructions, but burst out crying when she came up from her dip. By the end of the morning, the group of losers stood sorrowfully on the other side, a raggle-taggle group of kids who had failed the test. Kuku and Ritu, the pride of the Khot family, stood there too.

All the parents of the losers protested. Clearly they too had planned to enjoy their first cups of tea in peace, and that dream was now shattered. The instructors agreed to allow the losers to come in for water exercises and games in the shallow end, for the full price of swimming classes. Not one parent bargained or argued, and without further ado, our swimming classes began.

Every morning, we were coaxed out of bed by Aji at 4:30, while it was still dark outside. In the cool silence of our old bungalow, we made tea for ourselves and nibbled on the boiled eggs that Tulsi Bai had kept for us, while we waited for Uncle Srikanth to pick us up.

At the pool, Izzy and I walked to our separate Girls and Boys teams, did our warm-ups and learned how to hold our breath underwater and swim with the right movements, while Kuku and Ritu, along with the other losers, paddled or played dodge ball in the water.

As our swimming skills grew better, our instructors announced that the final test was coming up. What would we have to do to graduate from puppy paddlers to real swimmers? We'd have to dive off the highest board, land smoothly, and swim to the edge of the pool on your own. After our class was over, we trooped to the far end of the pool with our teams to examine the diving boards.

A tall concrete pillar towered above the deep end, with three diving boards at different levels. The lowest board was only a couple of feet above the surface while the middle board was at a nerve-wracking height of ten feet. We had to tip our heads back and crane our necks to look up at the highest board, looming far above us in the morning mist.

We had never seen anyone diving from that board except the quiet man whom everyone said was training for the Olympics. He came in every morning, as we were finishing our class and all of us stopped to watch him, including our instructors.

Unlike the others who came in and stood around the pool chatting with friends, this man never said a word to anyone. Unlike the others who splashed through their laps, he sliced through the water without a drop flying anywhere. All of us, including Izzy, wore frilly yellow swimming caps that tied under our chins, making us look like little Victorian ladies in bonnets, but he wore a black swim cap that fitted tightly around his shorn skull like a second layer of skin.

I shivered involuntarily as I looked at the board and then across the pool at Izzy. He had a nonchalant look on his face but nobody in his team was squabbling or laughing, so I knew they were scared too. Our instructors gave us a pep talk and showed us how to climb the ladder and walk on the bouncy diving board, one by one.

We mastered the lowest board fairly soon and a few days later, we were throwing ourselves off the middle board. As I climbed up the ladder to the middle board, I cast my eyes up the ladder and shivered, thanking my fates that I didn't have to dive off from that height today.

When the day arrived for our final test, Izzy and I could barely swallow our boiled eggs. We sat in the car with pale faces and refused to talk to Uncle Srikanth, envying Kuku and Ritu for their easy morning of doggy paddling with a tube.

After our warm-ups, our instructors walked us through the steps once again.

"Climb the ladder slowly and hold on with both hands. Remember that your feet are wet and the ladder is wet, so you must go carefully."

"Take slow and measured steps on the board. Remember that if you bounce, the board will bounce."

"Don't look around you when you're up there. Focus on the edge of the board."

"Whatever you do, don't land on your stomach in the water. That will hurt."

"When you go underwater, hold your breath, look around while you tread water, and then kick to come up."

"Remember to swim towards the side of the pool when you break the surface."

Our heads swam with the instructions. The instructors pushed us firmly towards the ladder.

"Remember the 1-2-3 move. What's the 1-2-3 move?"

We opened dry mouths and repeated the move dully. "One: Walk to the edge slowly and bend at the waist. Two: Reach forward to touch toes. Three: Lean forward and dive in with your head first."

"Very good. Now, let's begin. The Girls team will go first. Mahi, you'll go first."

I didn't hear anything after that. The instructor prodded me and I began to walk towards the foot of the ladder. My legs felt like jelly. I climbed three rungs of the ladder and looked around. Some of the parents had gathered to watch, clutching each other's arms in sympathy.

"Don't look down! Keep climbing. Look up! Look up!"

I climbed higher, passing the lowest board and then the medium board. I had never gone higher than this before. The metal bars of the ladder felt cold. As my head reached the highest board, I could hear the thudding of my heart in my ears. I knelt on the board, clutching the sides as tightly as I could.

"Stand up, Mahi! Stand up! Don't look down."

I peered over the edge of the board at my team. Everyone looked very far away and very small. My hands began to shake.

"Don't look down. You'll get scared."

"Stop talking to me if you don't want me to look down" I shouted back, furious at the instructor and at Aji for putting me up here. I looked over again to see if the instructor was feeling any remorse for putting my life at risk. Instead, after a heated debate with the instructor of the Boys team, he pulled on his swimming cap and began climbing up the ladder, shouting instructions to me.

"I'm coming up. Don't move."

I stood up quickly. I didn't want to be the baby who needed the instructor's help to dive. I dragged one foot in front of the other, walking steadily like they'd taught us, until I was at the edge. The board dipped ever so slightly with my weight.

I stretched my neck out to look into the water. The deep end was a menacing dark blue, not like the soft blue-green shallow end. I swallowed and looked around. The swimming pool was an open-air one, and the highest board towered over the walls. From my position, I could see people on scooters in the distance, trundling down the roads, blissfully unaware of my predicament. I wanted to shout to them to come and rescue me.

"Mahi! Come on! It's time to jump!"

I swung around as the instructor's voice boomed behind me, loud and terrifying in the silence. As my feet slipped on the wet surface and I lost my balance. I tried to do the 1-2-3 move, but it was too late. The board dipped, my knees jack-knifed, and I screamed as I was flipped into the air.

The next thing I knew, I was being fished out of the water with a long bamboo pole while the teams clapped for me. It was over. I clung to the edge of the pool, unable to pull myself over because my arms were shaking too much. The instructor patted my head and told me to stay in the water.

By the time my shattered pride had recovered, it was time for the Boys team to begin. I bobbed in the water, my eyes fixed on Izzy. He had seen my dive and I just knew he was going to mock me for the rest of my life.

But when Izzy started climbing the steps of the ladder, I straightened up quickly in the water. I saw his feet slip on the ladder a few times and I didn't have to hear his gasp to know how scared he was. I pulled myself out of the water and wrapped my towel around my shoulders, ready to hurry towards him, but the instructor held his arm out.

"No need to go there. Watch from here."

"But that's my brother!"

"I know. But you don't know anything. Let his teacher tell him what to do."

He was right, so I fell back and watched. Izzy's small round head bobbed as he climbed up the ladder and arrived at the highest board. He looked very small from where I was, inching along the board in his billowing swimming trunks.

He was so worried about his shorts coming off in the dive that he had pulled the string belt as tight as he could and tied a tight triple knot. He was very serious and his face was pale. An overwhelming sense of sympathy filled my heart and without thinking, I shouted up at him.

"Come on, Izzy! You can do it! Eye of the tiger!"

Izzy swivelled his head stiffly, not wanting to lose balance like I had, and looked down at me. I saw it in his eyes – the minute his brain registered how high up in the sky he was – and immediately regretted it.

Izzy cowered and began to back away from the edge. His instructor, who was standing on the far end, saw this and edged towards Izzy to grab him by the shoulders. Izzy tussled with him briefly and then the instructor frog-marched him along the board and pitched him into the deep end. Izzy rocketed into the water feet-first and disappeared into the blue.

I scanned the surface anxiously. It seemed like hours before his head appeared, the frilly cap hanging sideways. I gave a sigh of relief and rushed over to the side of the pool.

Izzy clung to the pole with all fours as the instructor fished him out and as I pulled him over the edge of the pool, he looked up at me and crowed triumphantly, "My shorts stayed on!"

CHAPTER THIRTEEN

Black Magic Frankie

Daddy returned from China with glowing reports of how well-mannered the children were. They cleaned their own school. They walked sedately in a line instead of whizzing past their parents into the traffic. They managed to eat without turning every meal into a food fight. We began to believe he was making up these paragons of virtue, but Aji listened to these stories with rapt attention, looking thoughtfully at us afterwards.

The subject of hiring a governess began to resurface in our tea time discussions and soon the search for a new one began.

A candidate was hired, but she left within two days. Two others were deemed extremely unsuitable by Aji. Another turned down the offer during the interview, deciding that she didn't want to live inside the Fort. And then, just when Daddy and Aji were about to give up, Frankie showed up.

This episode makes us shiver at how easily pure evil entered our home and our lives. For weeks afterwards, Aji would gather us close and cry at the thought of the horrible fate that almost befell her four precious *baabloos*. We rolled our eyes and submitted to her embraces then, but we do often wonder what could have happened that night if Aji and Tulsi Bai had not been so vigilant.

Nobody remembers where Frankie came from. He had been sent to us by a family friend who knew Daddy was looking for someone to mind the kids, and that was good enough. Frankie had a pointy narrow face and a scrawny neck, with big eyes spaced far apart, and always dressed in army fatigues. But he spoke well, could tell us long and fascinating stories, could converse with Daddy, was respectful to Aji, and seemed to be comfortable and confident in his new role. Daddy said maybe a governess was too tame for four boisterous kids, and someone like Frankie would be able to keep up with us.

Frankie was a bit of a drifter and didn't have a place to stay. He had just gotten off the bus from Goa, and claimed to have moved back from the Gulf recently. He moved into a room in the outhouse with just one plastic bag filled with his belongings, and very soon was entertaining us with all kinds of stories and jokes. The four of us took to him immediately, but Aji, who was fiercely protective, refused to let us be alone with Frankie at first.

Weeks passed and Kanappa began complaining about Frankie to Daddy. He didn't like Frankie but was unable to give anyone a real reason for his dislike. It was just an uneasy feeling, he said, but Daddy said he couldn't fire someone on a hunch, and so Frankie stayed.

Nobody accompanied us when we cycled along the quiet roads inside the Fort or clambered all over the crumbling walls of the ramparts. We romped through overgrown fields without being bothered by grown-ups about stray dogs or snakes. We chatted with strangers if they were doing something interesting, and if they had offered us food or chocolate, we would have accepted it in a heartbeat. But if Frankie was with us, Kanappa began to follow us like a shadow. We never knew whether this was on Aji's instructions or of his own accord.

One day, Frankie told us about a brilliant prank we were going to play on Kanappa. We couldn't come out of the house on our own at midnight, so Frankie had the most exciting role, but we could help prepare for it. There were piles of old magazines lying around in our book room and it took us the better part of an evening to cut out pictures of supermodels in swimsuits. At night, when Kanappa slept, tired from his day of honest labour, Frankie crept out and covered his front door with pictures of skimpily dressed women.

The next morning, when Kanappa returned from brushing his teeth, he found the door of his house covered with photographs of the swimsuit models. Kanappa was incensed and embarrassed, and he knew whom to blame. Frankie lived four doors down and acted innocent until Daddy was called in to put an end to the shouting.

While Daddy did ask Frankie to apologise, he didn't fire him as Kanappa expected. That was the beginning of a cold war between the two.

Torn between the two factions, we stopped listening to Kanappa and began to tease him instead. We pretended not to hear Kanappa when he told us not to stay so long in Frankie's room listening to stories. So instead of telling us, Kanappa would sit on the ground by Frankie's door, reminding us that we had to take our baths, do our homework, and eat dinner, until we got fed up with his mumbling and went home.

We knew what we were doing was wrong, but Frankie told us thrilling stories and made us feel like we were grown-ups while Kanappa treated us like we were kids.

Frankie had been hinting about a big secret, but refused to tell us anything more, no matter how much we pestered him. He waited for a chilly evening when we were making paper planes in Frankie's room and waiting for the Maggi noodles that were boiling on his single-flame burner. Kanappa sat on his haunches on the threshold, keeping an eye on us.

When Frankie told us it was time for us to hear about his secret, we were all agog. Our mouths fell open as he told us about his personal ghost, a spirit that was his best friend and watchman and who did all his work for him. Naturally we had hundreds of questions.

"Yes, yes. He does all my work. He washes my clothes, cooks my food, cleans my house." This must have been true because we had never seen Frankie doing any of those things.

"What does he look like, Frankie? Is he here now?" Ritu looked around Frankie's small room fearfully.

"No, no. He doesn't come out when there are people around. I've never seen him properly anyway. He comes out in the dark, while I'm sleeping, and even if I wake up at night, I pretend to keep my eyes closed so he doesn't get frightened. He's very shy."

"But what if he hurts you? Or what if he comes to our house to hurt us?"

"He won't hurt anyone unless I tell him to, and I'd never tell him to hurt you."

Izzy looked puzzled. "But is he a good ghost or a bad ghost?"

"He's a good ghost, but if someone troubles me, he becomes a bad ghost."

Frankie lived in a small room in the outhouse. He had taken down the bright tube lights that were put up, claiming they gave him a headache. A bare bulb dangled from a wire in the corner, emitting a weak orange light that left all the corners of the rooms in darkness. Usually we liked how cosy and secret it looked, but Frankie's eyes looked very dark at this moment.

Izzy was still curious. "How do you tell him what to do if you can't look at him?"

"Well, he reads my mind, you see. I don't have to tell him anything. He knows what I'm thinking."

"How?" Ritu breathed.

"He's part of my spirit, attached to my soul," said Frankie. "When I think of something, he thinks of it too."

"Like telepathy?" I asked.

Frankie nodded and leaned forward. "You want to see how I control the ghost? But if I show you, you can't tell anyone, okay?"

We nodded. Frankie rolled up the sleeve of his army jacket. High up on his thin arm, there was an ugly bumpy scar. "See this? It looks like there's something under the skin, right? That's how I control him."

"What is it?"

"It's a small plastic bag, filled with a little bit of my hair and a little bit of the ghost's hair."

"How did it get there?"

"Ah, now you're getting too deep into the secret." Frankie smiled mysteriously and acted as if he was about to get up.

"No, tell us. Please tell us!" we screamed at him, desperate to hear the end of the story. Frankie sat down again and continued without skipping a beat.

"Many years ago, when I was in Goa, I was down on my luck. I didn't have any money. I was sleeping on the beach at night because I didn't have a house. I couldn't buy any food to eat. I was very sad, so I sat on the sand and cried, looking at the ocean. I saw an old man walking out of the water and when he approached me, I sat up and wiped my tears. He started speaking kindly to me and it was only much later that I realised his clothes were completely dry, even though he had just come out of the ocean."

We *oohed* and *aahed*, but Kuku scooted closer to me and wrapped her clammy fingers around my arm.

"We chatted for a while and then the old man took me to a restaurant to buy me my first meal in days. That's when he told me about the ghost. He said it was a full moon night that night, and if I brought him some special things, he could summon a ghost for me who would solve all my problems. And he did. I brought him everything he asked for, and he lit a fire on the beach and started praying. There was a lot of smoke, and I must have fainted during the ceremony because when I woke up it was morning, and the man was gone! And guess what was on my arm?"

We couldn't even say the words, because we were so enthralled.

"This bump. The man had told me it would be there, and a little bit of my hair was missing. And then I realised I had the ghost nearby. After that, the ghost found me a room, made food for me every day, and cleaned my house. It even got me money if I needed it."

Izzy blinked and closed his mouth slowly. Izzy's one task was to wipe the table after dinner, and he hated doing that. "I wish I had my own ghost."

Frankie looked at him. "Oh, but you can!"

We stared at Frankie, disbelieving him. There was no way that it could be so easy. We began to talk at the same time, but Frankie shushed us and leaned forward.

"All you have to do is come here when the moon is full. Late at night, after everyone has gone to sleep. You have to bring one litre of milk and a box of something sweet to offer to the spirits. You have to bring a blade and a bottle of Dettol. I'll arrange a fire, and we'll have to cut off a bit of your hair."

"And you'll put it under our skin in a plastic bag?" asked Ritu. "What if Aji sees it?"

"We'll make the cut at the back of your neck, under your hair. And for you Izzy, we'll put it on your back. Then it'll always be covered up."

"Can we get a ghost for Pinky too?"

"No, everyone can't have one because then you won't be special. I'm only doing this for the four of you because you asked for it so much. Once you have your ghost, you can decide if you want to share it with Pinky, but you can't tell anyone till the ceremony is over. Not Aji, not Tulsi Bai, not Pinky, nobody. Do you promise?"

We made a pact to do as Frankie said. The full moon was two days away, and we started making big plans. For the next 48 hours, we were so full of excitement that we couldn't contain ourselves, but this seemed like the kind of secret that Daddy and Aji wouldn't like at all. We had been sworn to secrecy, and had promised we wouldn't tell Zayra and Aaliya or Pinky. Wild horses couldn't have dragged the secret from us.

On the day of the big ceremony, we begged for *jalebis* and then refused to eat them when Kanappa brought them back from the market. We checked that there was milk in the fridge and Dettol in the bathroom. We climbed onto the shelf where Daddy kept his razors and checked that there were extras.

By the evening of the ceremony, we were almost delirious with excitement. Aji asked us to sit down to do our homework, so we bent our heads over our books and whispered to each other.

"By this time tomorrow, our ghosts will be doing our homework for us. We'll never have to do homework again."

"Do you think it'll hurt when he puts the plastic bag of hair under our skin?"

"It might hurt a bit but you have to be brave if you want to get something. Remember how Rambo stitches up his own arm?"

"How are we going to climb over Daddy when he's sleeping? What if he wakes up?"

We had arranged with Frankie that we would drop off the milk and other items before dinner so he could prepare for the ceremony. That would be the hard part, because Aji's chair was right next to the kitchen. But between the four of us, we thought we could manage.

I put the packet of milk under my sweater, while Izzy tucked the box of *jalebis* into the waistband of his pants. We walked out of the kitchen as casually as we could and were three feet from the door when Tulsi Bai asked us what we were up to. Thinking quickly, I said that we were taking milk for the dogs, but then Aji noticed Ritu. Ritu had the bottle of Dettol under her nightie, and she was holding it away from her like it was a bomb about to explode.

As it turned out, it didn't require wild horses to drag the secret from us; just a few severe questions from our usually indulgent grandmother. She called for Daddy frantically and he rushed in, alarmed by the shrill note of urgency in her voice.

He listened carefully to the story, his eyes running over the evidence all lined up in front of him: razor blades, Dettol, a packet of milk, and *jalebis*.

Now that Daddy was in charge, Aji started weeping, horrified at the thought of what might have been planned for us that night.

We were sent to our room and told to shut the door and stay inside. Daddy and Aji murmured together in a serious tone for a while, and then we heard the door slam as Daddy marched towards Frankie's house.

By now we were quaking in our socks, because we'd eavesdropped on the conversation and heard serious things like 'devil worship', 'criminal', and the worst of them all, 'I told you so.'

We took our baths and ate our dinner in silence that night, listening to the raised voices coming from outside. All the other families that lived in the outhouse had come out to witness the drama and clutch their children close, but the four of us were shepherded into our bedroom by Tulsi Bai and told to go to sleep.

The next morning, Frankie and his belongings had disappeared. Izzy speculated with a thrilled shiver that Daddy had shot him and thrown his body in the well, but since we didn't have a gun in the house, this was ruled out.

Aji just cried when we asked about Frankie. Tulsi Bai would hunch an impatient shoulder and pretend she hadn't heard.

We were too scared to ask Daddy, but when we asked Kanappa, we got the whole story delivered in a victorious manner, with all the embellishments we could have wanted.

"I always knew he was a rotten apple. I always knew it! He was up to no good! I told your father. I told your grandmother. He wasn't fit to look after you all. Filling your heads with such nonsense! Ha! Do you know what his room looked like when we went in? He had made a fire and he had lined up knives on the side of his room. Imagine what could have happened that night if he had succeeded. You could all be dead right now! The whole Khot family, wiped out in one night by that man. He's lucky we didn't call the police. What? What do you mean, what happened to him? Your father told him to get all his stuff and leave, and I threw his clothes out with my own hands! I walked behind him all the way to the gate of the Fort, just to make sure he really left. Thirty minutes of walking on a cold night with my old knees. But I didn't want him to come back here. He'll never come back to Belgaum if he knows what's good for him. Ha!"

After Frankie's departure, Daddy never spoke of governesses again.

CHAPTER FOURTEEN

Fireworks in the Fort

If the monsoon made a dramatic entrance into our lives, winter always crept up softly, sending gentle reminders before beginning in earnest so we were always prepared. When the morning mist started to hang in the air for a little longer every morning, Aji made sure that our winter clothes and blankets were unpacked and sunned, ready for the sudden chill that was about to descend on us.

At night, the *raat ki rani* bush at our gate sent tendrils of fragrance all the way into our bedrooms. In the mornings, when we went to school, our breath came out in small white puffs. We liked to put our pencils in our mouth and pretend we were smoking pipes and blowing out clouds of smoke, which always sent the nuns into fits of disapproval.

Winter in Belgaum was always fun, especially in an old bungalow like ours. Our beds were piled high with thick blankets and we wore socks while we slept. In the morning, Aji pulled her shawl closer and declared that this was the coldest winter she'd ever faced. The cats became extra clingy and were always trying to creep under our sweaters for a cuddle. Even our dogs were unwilling to rise from the warm beds of cardboard, newspaper, and jute sacks that we made for them.

When we were very little, Daddy used to put a bucket of hot water near the bathroom sink, because we refused to brush our teeth in the freezing water. However, now that we were all grown up, we began to use tap water and *brrrr* our way through brushing our teeth.

But winter meant Christmas parties, Santa Claus, ten days off from school, building the Old Man to burn at midnight on New Year's Eve, and a house filled with cake and party snacks. It also meant dinner parties with *dabga* and bonfires.

It was well into winter when one day, Kanappa brought in a massive earthenware pot and plonked it on the kitchen platform. Ritu was floating about in the kitchen trying to smuggle milk for the new kittens, and she came running to us to deliver her news. We all knew what the pot meant in winter. A *dabga* party!

The four of us loved a good *dabga*. There was something so exciting about the whole process. Kanappa filled the earthen pot with raw winter vegetables: purple sweet potatoes as big as Kuku's foot, sweet baby carrots that tasted like you'd dipped them in honey, tender peas in the pod, beans that snapped with freshness, and for flavour, whole onions and big cloves of garlic. He stuffed the narrow opening of the pot with straw and put it in a hole in the ground. We lit a blazing bonfire over it at the start of the party, and by the time the bonfire died down to ashes, the vegetables were baked and ready.

Kanappa pulled out the pot, black and charred after being under a roaring bonfire, and pulled out the vegetables. Roasted in their own juices to a buttery soft texture, these vegetables were the tastiest we'd ever known, and were delicious with a squeeze of lime juice on top.

To accompany this, a tub full of chicken had been marinated and the *tandoor* that Daddy built was being fired up. Aji was sorting through a bushel of sweet winter carrots that had just been delivered from the market, and chatting with Tulsi Bai about making *gajar halwa*. We were ecstatic already – it was going to be a good evening.

While I called our friends and begged their parents for permission for them to stay over, Kuku and Ritu disappeared to Zayra and Aaliya's house to do the same. We spent most of the day interfering in the party preparations.

The four of us got under everyone's feet as tables were moved outside, a makeshift bar was set up, and speakers for music were connected. Kanappa batted us away when we tried to get a nibble of the vegetables he was putting into the *dabga*, and then looked around suspiciously.

"Where's your brother? He's usually always here for this."

We shrugged.

"Go and find him. Go ask Tulsi Bai where he is."

We wandered away, stopping to play with the kittens for a while. It must have been an hour or so later when we realised that Izzy really was missing. We split up to look for him, and I found him rolling about on the couch in the living room, clutching his belly. His face was screwed up in pain, and he was moaning softly to himself.

When I called Aji over, she took one look at him and made a phone call to Uncle Zaheer. All of us hovered around Izzy, wringing our hands. We have scars that have lasted for decades, left over from our wrestling matches. We scratched and pinched each other, we pulled hair and punched noses, and we thought nothing of it. But we couldn't bear the sight of each other unwell. The only thing that was allowed to knock us down was one of us.

Uncle Zaheer arrived and placed his long cool fingers on Izzy's forehead, then palpated his belly. Izzy moaned again. Uncle Zaheer rolled Izzy around to put the stethoscope to his back, and we saw a small pile of half-eaten carrots under a cushion.

"Izzy, how many of these have you eaten?" Uncle Zaheer asked sternly.

Izzy looked at Aji sheepishly and she gasped. She rushed off into the room where the sweet carrots had been stored and came back with shock on her face.

"He's eaten at least 30," she gasped. "Big ones. Full size."

Uncle Zaheer laughed as he pulled out a bottle from his bag. Izzy had snuck into the room and gorged on the sweet carrots. "You know what's happening to you, Izzy? All the carrots are turning into gas and filling up your stomach like a big balloon right now. I'm going to give you…."

"Is he going to burst like a balloon, Uncle Zaheer?" Kuku looked terrified.

"No, no, he's going to be fine." Then he caught the message in Aji's eyes and amended his statement. "He might have burst, if I hadn't got here in time. You have to be very careful when you're stealing food – you never know what might go wrong."

We nodded gravely, watching as Uncle Zaheer poured medicine into a spoon and administered it to Izzy. He sent Izzy off to the toilet with a warning to stay there until everything came out, and then sat down for a cup of tea with Aji, waiting to see if Izzy needed anything else.

Twenty minutes later, Izzy emerged from the bathroom wreathed in smiles, having created noises in there that could've scared the birds off the roof. Uncle Zaheer left some medicine behind, assured us that Izzy would be fine for the party but must never steal food again, and disappeared.

As evening fell, the fairy lights were switched on. Someone tested music on the speakers. Mahua arrived and was swept away by me to see the kittens. Pinky was dropped off by her patient father. Zayra and Aaliya walked over in their party clothes. Once Izzy had told everyone about his carrot emergency in great detail, many times over, our attention shifted to the evening plans. Izzy and I had planned this one a long time ago.

"We're going to light firecrackers outside Uncle Hani's window. They won't even know it's us." I told everyone.

"It's a covert operation," cackled Izzy. He had obviously been watching too much *Rambo* again. "We're going to infiltrate their bungalow."

"Yes" breathed Kuku, Ritu, and Pinky as one.

Mahua looked doubtful. "I think they'll know it's us."

Izzy brushed it off. "It doesn't matter. If they ask us, we'll deny it. They can't do anything if we don't admit to it." Faced with that logic, Mahua agreed, and the plan was afoot.

Uncle Hani was Zayra and Aaliya's grandfather and Uncle Zaheer's father. He wrinkled his nose when he looked at us, as if we were smelly, and he referred to us (and his own grandchildren) as *'bekaar bachche'*. He was also suspicious of us, as if we were always up to some mischief. Which, to be fair, was exactly what we were up to at that moment.

He slept in the corner room of their bungalow, which was close enough to the gate that we could light a string of crackers and fling it right outside his window. Zayra and Aaliya participated in this activity as if they didn't live in the same house, and pretended to their family that they didn't know who threw crackers into their yard every time the Khots had a party.

Although Zayra and Aaliya were our neighbours, the bungalows inside our old Fort were spaced far apart. This meant that even though we all referred to their house as "next door", their bungalow was ten minutes away from ours. To get to their house, we had to run past our own garden, on a dark, dimly-lit road, risking our lives against snakes, rabid dogs, and vehicles driving at full speed. As far as we were concerned, we were also risking kidnappers, headless ghosts and other supernatural nasties.

But this was one of our favourite party tricks, and we would take on anything to do it. We sent the smallies ahead to take the excitable dogs and settle down in the waiting spot. Because we were using fire and explosives, they were allowed to watch this prank but not participate in it. Mahua and I went off with Izzy to locate the firecrackers, matches and all the other contraband that we would need.

Kuku and Ritu took Pinky and crept past the Sunken Garden where all the grown-ups were seated. They slipped out of the gate and onto the dark road. The road ran straight past our gate and turned off to the right, and the Hani bungalow was the first bungalow on the other side of the turn. Our waiting spot was an overgrown patch of bushes right in the middle of the turn. From here, we could see both bungalows clearly, and more importantly, we could watch as all hell broke loose in the Hani house after the crackers went off.

The smell of tandoori chicken wafted through our garden, and the sound of laughter and clinking glasses filled the air. Izzy, Mahua and I dashed to the waiting spot and found that Rum and Raisin were almost fainting with excitement. So were the smallies. We had to issue strict instructions to make them settle down.

"Don't even try to run with us or we'll beat you."

"Don't TOUCH the firecrackers or you'll get gunpowder on your clothes. Then we'll have to wash you."

"Don't you go blabbing to everyone about this or we'll beat you."

"Don't giggle and make noise here, or the grown-ups will see us."

"When we tell you to run back, you run back, okay?"

"If you don't listen to us, we'll beat you."

Once everyone had agreed to the rules, we crouched in a circle to prepare. Izzy ripped the covering off the crackers and then, licking his gunpowder-covered fingertips, began to peel the wick back so it would light fast and burn quick. I pulled out the matches and examined them to see that they were dry and ready to burn. Then Mahua and I hot-footed it to the Hani bungalow to make sure the coast was clear.

A few seconds later, Izzy ran towards us, bent over low so as not to be spotted. He saw that Mahua and I were clutching each other and breathing fast, our eyes glittering. Recognising the signs of an oncoming giggling fit, he pinched us hard and muttered a threat through gritted teeth, so we gulped it down and nodded that the coast was clear.

We did one last surveillance of the bungalow – all quiet, lights off, TV on in the interiors of the house – and looked around to see if the smallies were watching. One small hand emerged from the bushes and gave us a thumbs-up.

Izzy swung his throwing arm to warm up, cracked his neck and knuckles, and nodded at me. We sat up on our toes, ready to run, and I struck a match. Izzy held the wick of the crackers to the flame, and it fizzed and ignited. He hurled it over the bushes into the bungalow, where it landed perfectly, right outside the window.

We waited just long enough to make sure the flame was burning down the wick, and then ran as fast as we could to the dark corner where the smallies were, just as the string of crackers began to explode. The sound of the bursting crackers echoed in the silence of the Fort, propelling us even faster to our hiding place.

This was always our favourite moment. It felt like we were in a movie, with bombs exploding in the background and sending up a fiery cloud of smoke and flame as we ran. Mahua and I dived into the bushes and ducked down low. Izzy leapt up into the air at the last minute, arms and legs flailing, landing in the bushes on top of the smallies and the dogs and knocking the air out of them all. It was an impressive move and I stored it in my head for the next time.

We crouched in the bushes, eagerly waiting for the ruckus to begin in the Hani bungalow. The lights in the verandah were switched on. We heard voices. *We'd disturbed the household.* We cackled and desperately covered our mouths to stifle any sounds. Someone appeared in the doorway. *This was a roaring success! Was he brandishing a stick? Was the stick for us? Oh, the glory of it all!* We held our breath as the man walked around the gate, looking up and down the road, and then breathed a sigh of relief as he went back inside and turned off the lights.

Glowing with perspiration and success, we slipped back inside the house, just in time to see Kanappa unpacking the *dabga*. We squatted around him to watch. Unpacking the *dabga* was a spectacle that even the grown-ups liked to witness. He pulled it out from under the ashes of the bonfire, handling it deftly with a damp cloth and light fingers. He wiped it down, lay it on its side over a plate, and pulled the steaming plug of straw out with a *pock* sound. A cloud of vegetable-scented steam puffed out into the cold winter night.

Soon we were sitting around the bonfire with our plates on our laps. If we'd been paying attention, we would have noticed the hubbub at the gate of our bungalow, but we were hungry and the sweet potato was perfect if you put just the right amount of lemon and salt on it.

It was only when we heard the all-too familiar voice that we looked up. Uncle Hani had walked over in his night *kurta pyjama* to tell Daddy what we had done. We sighed and stood up to apologise, potatoes bulging in our cheeks, listening to his booming *"Bekaaaar bachhhe"* echo across the garden.

CHAPTER FIFTEEN

The Great Christmas Horror Show

As the first day of December dawned in the Fort, the usual bustle in the Khot house turned into frenzied activity. We dived into the Christmas spirit early and with great gusto. We dusted off our Neil Diamond audio cassettes and played Christmas carols at full volume, every morning and evening. We spent days putting up our tree and baubles, planting real grass in our elaborate Nativity scene, and optimistically putting up giant red stockings all around the house for Santa to fill.

But what we really looked forward to was the Christmas party, which was the highlight of our year. What started as a small party for us and our friends had turned into a full-blown extravaganza over the years, and each year we added something new. By the time I was eleven years old, we arranged plays and puppet shows, a wild Treasure Hunt, and thrilling mazes and games that took days to set up. Of course, Santa's entrance got bigger and more dramatic every year, and this year, we were adding pyrotechnics and sound effects.

From November onwards, kids in school began to ask us when the invitations would be handed out. Aji received frantic calls from parents who shared the phone with their heavy breathing child, checking that they were on the list for the party. Daddy and Aji made endless lists, and the four of us spent a whole weekend making the invitations by hand.

With well over a hundred invitations to be written out and elaborately decorated with glitter glue, marker pens and cotton wool snow, making the invitations and sending them out was a painstaking task. We recruited our friends to help, and this was the first task that we had to complete. Mahua with her neat, round handwriting, and Zayra with her precise artistry had the most important roles, but everyone got a task.

Every year, we had a family committee meeting in which we decided a theme for the party. Daddy nimbly dodged the themes we suggested at first – rabbits, Rambo, cats, and cake – and guided us firmly towards more appropriate ideas.

In 1994, when Surat was devastated by the plague, we used bamboo and *papier mache* to build a giant rat, as big as a real life elephant, and hoisted it onto a metal stand on top of our pool. The next year, we chose to highlight the preservation of wildlife, so we built an eight-foot tall panda. Building these characters took weeks and the joint efforts of the four of us, as well as Mahua, Pinky, and Zayra and Aaliya, plus anyone else who showed up.

For the four of us, the lead-up to the party was as much fun as the party itself.

The Treasure Hunt was the biggest attraction of the party. This was the only part of the party that the kids didn't help with. We weren't allowed to participate in planning the clues, so that we could play with everyone else on the day of the party. Daddy invited volunteer grown-ups to come over, and we were locked into the house for the whole day while they decided on locations for the clues.

Every year, we were grouped into two teams: Girls versus Boys. The Treasure was always a big box of Cadbury's Dairy Milk chocolate bars, wrapped in glittering gold. And every year, the grown-ups seemed to delight in hiding it in impossible-to-reach locations.

Last year, the Treasure had been wrapped in plastic and sunk to the bottom of the swimming pool. The Girls team was ahead by a few seconds, and Mahua and I stood by the side of the pool, trying to figure out how to get it out. The pool was filled with algae because it had been too cold to swim in it for weeks now, and there were usually frogs under the algae.

But then we saw the Boys team galloping in from the gate with determined looks on their faces. Mahua squeaked in horror, and before I knew it, I had leapt onto the rim of the pool. I dived through the algae and the frogs to retrieve the Treasure from the bottom of the murky pool and emerged a hero.

The year before that, the Treasure had been hidden in Zayra and Aaliya's garden. Uncle Zaheer had gamely given Daddy the go-ahead for this and had kept the secret from his family. When we figured out the clue, Zayra and Aaliya screamed in chagrin that it had been there the whole time.

Uncle Hani was sitting peacefully in his garden chair, reading the newspaper and warming his old bones in the evening sun when a herd of children stampeded through the gate. He got up speedily to ward us off, but nobody could have stopped us.

Eighty children trampled over his carefully tended gladioli and rose beds while Uncle Hani stood by and watched sadly. When we spotted the Treasure in the azure fountain, ten kids with muddy shoes jumped in. A riot broke out between the Girls and the Boys team and the Treasure was ripped apart in the ensuing chaos, leaving everyone with scraps of the box and broken bits of chocolate.

As he watched us thundering off his property, Uncle Hani shook his head and mumbled *"Bekaar bachhe"* for the hundredth time that month.

While Daddy and the volunteers were in charge of the clues for the Treasure Hunt, they also set up the other games, strung up a Golden Pot filled with chocolates for a blindfolded kid to break open, and wrote the skit.

We volunteered, we did the papering and building of giant rats and pandas, we helped with the cake, and we spent two days separating toys and sweets into individual goodie bags. But the piece de resistance of our party for us was our Horror Show. This was left entirely to us, and we gave it everything we had.

The Horror Show started as a side attraction at our first party. That year Daddy had brought home one of those ball-shaped lights that sparked electricity to your fingertips if you touched it. We thought it would be exciting to have a fortune teller read from it and we asked Aunty Olga, a spirited and fun Russian lady who had married and settled in Belgaum with her family, to play the part.

We cleaned out Daddy's old van, draped it with gauzy curtains, and dim red lights, and burned incense in it to make it seem mysterious. Aunty Olga designed her own costume and embellished it with mirrors and beads and scarves. On the day of the party, when she pulled open the door of the van to reveal the lair inside, everyone (including all of us who had made it) were gobsmacked. People lined up to get their fortune told from the magic ball, and it was a smashing success.

The next year, we decided to use the van again, but this time, inspired by Indiana Jones, we decorated it like the inside of an Egyptian tomb. We chose Bunty, a family friend who was about 6.5 feet tall to be our Egyptian Mummy. Because he was so big, we underestimated the number of gauze rolls it would require to cover him, and Kanappa was sent to the chemist multiple times.

Finally Bunty was wrapped, rolled in the mud to get the centuries-of-dust-and-decay look, and helped into the van. Each time a kid peeked in, Bunty would gurgle and raise his stiff arms towards the child, sending many of them away in terrified tears. It was a roaring success, and from that year onwards, the Horror Show was a fixture at our parties.

As we got older and more capable of managing our own stunts, we decided to go bigger. This year, we had planned a Tea Party of Ghouls. Mahua, Izzy and I were the masterminds of this event.

We rolled the van into the shed at the side of the house and draped dark cloth, bedsheets and curtains all over the shed to create dark passages. Inside the van, we set the stage for a gruesome tea party.

Pinky was the Floating Head and stuck her head through a hole made in a curtain. Aaliya and Kuku were mini Egyptian Mummies, and this time it took only three rolls of gauze to wrap their diminutive forms. Zayra and Ritu were witches, with their faces covered in green eye-shadow from an old make-up kit.

On the table, we laid out a teapot and cups. We made a mould of Maggi noodles, slathered it in ketchup, and called it Brain Salad.

Pinky's mother, who was an expert baker, made small cakes that were iced to look like dismembered fingers.

The gene for atmospherics came through in all of Daddy's kids, and we spent a considerable amount of time planning how we would achieve a perfectly scary and sinister mood. As our curious visitors entered, the wicked laugh from Michael Jackson's Thriller played on loop on hidden speakers.

Mahua and I were going to usher the kids into the drapery of dark cloth at the entrance of the shed. Izzy was hidden amidst the curtains, and was going to lightly brush a damp towel over the faces of those who passed, to imitate the musty wings of a bat flying past. The kids would move on to the door of the van, where they could witness the ghouls partaking of a deliciously creepy feast, and then they would be escorted out by us.

It was the perfect plan.

But for all our effort, the Horror Show descended into chaos very soon after it began. Over 70 kids thronged the entrance, desperate to see what was hidden from their view. Mahua and I scolded and pushed back, but the kids stormed through the flimsy barricade that we set up and began to flounder through the dark curtains.

Izzy was panicked by the rush of kids and knew he wouldn't be able to lightly brush all of them. Instead he began to wave the wet towel about wildly, smacking kids on the face. When he realised that a lot of the kids were too short to get the towel in the face, he crouched down and started slapping the towel on the backs of their legs.

By the time the startled kids recovered from the wet towel assault, they arrived at the door of the van where they stood gaping at the tea party. When faced by a large and wondering audience, the smallies felt like they had to put on a show that involved more than tamely nibbling scary snacks.

The witches shrieked curses and leaped up and down. Pinky shook the curtains, rolled her eyes up to show the white eyeballs and groaned loudly. The Egyptian Mummies, forgetting that they were supposed to be inanimate, rose up and began to screech and hurl noodles at the kids.

Mahua and I were alarmed at the horrible sounds coming from within, but we stood our ground and fielded questions from the anxious parents who waited with us. Unearthly noises echoed from behind the dark drapes. The ghouls moaned and groaned, and the children who went in screamed and cried, and Michael Jackson's zombie laugh rang out over our heads over and over again.

The first batch of kids emerged wild-eyed from their traumatic experience, thoroughly shaken and completely bewildered.

They didn't know they had experienced the underside of bat wings or seen Brain Salad. Instead, they had gotten lost in a tangle of curtains, been smacked on their legs and faces with wet towels, and had noodles dangling off their heads. Some of them were crying.

The parents fell upon their children, patting and consoling, wiping their running noses and picking bits of food out of their hair. Mahua and I, the only ones around from the organizing committee, held our breath and waited for the reproaches.

One fond mother pushed her way to the front of the crowd to grip her son's upper arm. "What's happening in there, Sonu?"

But Sonu just shook his head and gulped. Sonu was a pale, timid kid whose soft knees were unsullied by scabs and scars. We didn't think much of him. His mother glared at us as she brushed Sonu's hair off his forehead.

"Look at this! He can't stop shivering with fear. I'm taking him home right now. I think you should stop this."

Some of the other parents nodded and began to pull their kids away, out of the line that waited to go in. But at this, a roar of defiance went up from the kids. They were terrified by the noises, but they were most certainly not going to miss out on whatever was going on behind those curtains.

Sonu pulled back. "No Ayi, Ayi… I'm not going home. I want to go in again."

"No, Sonu *beta*," his mother insisted. "You'll have bad dreams… you know you…"

But Sonu took a deep breath, wrenched himself free from his mother's pinching grip, and marched up to us.

A surge of other kids followed him, yanking the noodles off their shoulders and brushing tears away with the backs of their hands.

Mahua and I looked at the parents and then at the kids. We shrugged and held the curtain open, and they walked into the screaming darkness for a second wet-towel thrashing.

CHAPTER SIXTEEN

The Egyptian Mummy Returns

Power cuts were a big part of our lives in the 80s and 90s, and when Daddy tried to tell us how poor kids studied with candles and still got better marks than us, we were able to retort that we often studied in candle light too. Those were the days of load shedding, when the electricity was turned off at scheduled times so that the Electricity Department could preserve power and distribute it more efficiently.

For us, it meant planning our bath time around the schedule and leaning over our dinner plates so that Eclipse couldn't steal our fried fish in the dark. We had learnt the latter the hard way.

On this cold winter evening, it was bath-time in the Khot house. Kuku and Ritu fished out the last mugs of hot water from big buckets and sluiced it over their heads, chatting while they towelled their hair. They looked like twins, completed each other's sentences, spoke with the same singsong intonation; and they did everything together, including taking baths.

It had been a good evening so far. Daddy was out at a dinner party and wouldn't be back till late. Aji was hosting an old friend of hers, so they were busy with cups of tea and soup, and we had been relatively unsupervised.

So far, we had held an all-out food fight at dinner, catapulting beans into each other's plates or at each other's heads from our spoons. We had eaten two bowls of ice-cream each and were thinking about sneaking a third.

At homework time, instead of putting our noses in our books and studying, we had held our popular Desk Sale, in which the four of us bartered precious items from our desks with each other.

Ritu squirreled away all her treasures and usually had the most pristine items for exchange: a lockable diary with kittens on the cover, a set of unbroken Camlin crayons, and most precious of all, sheets of gemstone-like stickers.

But this time, it was Izzy who had made a killing. He'd been making his own perfumes lately, mixing *attar* and water and Daddy's aftershave in little bottles, and all three of us wanted one. Izzy had bargained hard and won himself an almost-new fountain pen, a Danish coin with a hole in the centre, and a packet of cola-flavoured candy that popped in your mouth.

Now he was standing on a stool in front of the mirror, his towel around his waist, combing his wet hair carefully into spikes and humming tunelessly.

Without any warning, the lights went out and our house descended into chaos. Kuku and Ritu screamed, purely for effect and not because they were scared. Izzy leapt off his stool, shouting that he would get the candles, and skidded off into the dark. The ensuing crashes told us he was either knocking over chairs or battling wildebeest in the dining room.

Aji called from the drawing room to check on us and I put down my book with a sigh. There was never a moment of peace in this house. The smallies, at 6 and 7 years of age, were just short enough to get underfoot in the most inconvenient manner. Daddy was worried they would trip Aji over in the dark, so they had strict instructions to freeze whenever the lights went out.

Once everyone had been supplied with candles, the four of us gathered to eat our third helping of ice cream. Izzy's eyes glittered in the golden glow of the candle as he suggested we take the Eygptian Mummy mask out for a spin and scare some people.

We were still a little scared of the mask, and with no lights on in our compound or the surrounding bungalows, we decided not to go too far from the house. In our backyard, if we squeezed under a lemon tree with very sharp thorns, we could cross into the neighbour's compound, where there was a whole outhouse full of people who had not yet seen the mask.

We crept out of the house in the dark with the mask and the robe under our arms, looking back to make sure Aji didn't see us. Once outside, the dogs bounced up to accompany us and we didn't feel quite so scared.

The four of us jumped up and down near the lemon tree to scare away snakes, then got down on our bellies and squirmed under it, with the dogs squirming beside us, until we all emerged in the neighbour's compound.

A deep well with a bucket and pulley marked the boundary between our properties, and the cavernous mouth yawned dark and wide. After our favourite peacock had fallen in and drowned the previous year, we were very careful of this well. Weaving a wide circle around it, we tucked ourselves into the hedge and settled down on the ground to survey the scene.

About 200 feet away, the women of the outhouse stood in frilly nighties, chatting amicably with each other. After their families had been fed and the day's chores completed, they gathered here to exchange news and take a break. Some of them sat on their doorsteps, picking stones out of rice for the next day.

The kids milled about beside them, drawing figures on the ground with sticks, pushing their luck before they were shouted at to go to bed. A couple of men hung about, smoking or staring up at the stars.

But the only one who worried us was Pappu, who stood cleaning his scooter, dressed in an old vest and a pair of striped shorts held up with a *naada*. Pappu ruled the outhouse, and was Kanappa's close friend and advisor. He knew everything about everything, and could tell us what to do with a dead snake or how to get rid of the beehives that hung from our trees. He also didn't take kindly to the kind of antics we had planned for tonight, and we were sure he wasn't the type to hesitate before smacking us.

We weighed our options. The women and children were easy prey, but Pappu's presence might make them feel braver. However, we had come all the way and so we decided to do it anyway. We dressed Izzy in the robe, pulled the mask on over his small round head, and then threw ourselves back into the bushes nearby to watch the fun.

Izzy began to hop from one foot to the other, moaning in a ghoulish manner. First the dogs of the outhouse twitched their ears and sat up, looking this way and that. The women were next. They hushed each other and looked around. Pappu was bending to wipe the grease off his scooter when they began shrieking, and he straightened up hastily.

The women screamed, pointing and clutching each other while the kids stood transfixed, sticks still in their hands.

Izzy, goaded on by this satisfactory result, began to dance even harder, his ghostly groans getting louder. Pappu grabbed a stick from a kid and started forward as if to teach the ghost a lesson, but then stopped in his tracks. He stood there and watched, noting the diminutive height of this threatening apparition, the bushes shaking with glee, and the Khot dogs standing nearby, panting and wagging their tails.

Pappu turned to the womenfolk and shot out a few words. They lapsed into silence, rolled their eyes and tutted, and went back to their rice cleaning. The kids were still mesmerised by the dance. Pappu pulled up a plastic chair, sat down and folded his arms across his big belly, and continued looking in our direction.

Izzy wasn't sure what to do. "Why's he sitting there?" he puffed, continuing to hop. "What should I do? I don't think he's scared."

"Of course he's scared. Otherwise he would come out here to shout at us" I hissed. "Keep going. Don't stop."

Encouraged, Izzy hopped on, waving his arms like a rampaging tiger. Pappu continued to stare in our direction. It was dark and we couldn't tell for sure, but I don't think he even blinked. The women finished cleaning the rice and began to disperse, taking one last look at the small dancing Egyptian Mummy and shaking their heads.

Kuku sensed that we were losing our audience. "Izzy, do something else! You can't keep doing the same dance."

Izzy racked his brains to think of his next move. We had recently watched *Mary Poppins* for the hundredth time, and were teaching ourselves the tap dance routine of the chimney sweeps. Izzy put his hands on his hips and began to kick his legs smartly, stamping his feet instead of tapping because he was wearing chappals. We were satisfied with this and turned to see if Pappu was impressed. He wasn't.

"I don't think Pappu's seen *Mary Poppins*, Izzy. Try something Indian" hissed Ritu.

Izzy loved the dance that drunk men did in front of the Ganpati procession, and he didn't need prompting. He put his hands behind his head, bent his knees, and gyrated his hips in wild circles. Pappu had probably danced in front of a procession at some point, and we were sure this would strike a chord for him. But Pappu stayed put, expressionless even from a distance.

Izzy was starting to pant now. The robe was hot and thick, and the mask had tiny holes for the nostrils, so it barely allowed any air in. "What do I do? What do I do?"

We didn't quite know what to suggest. "Let's go home, Izzy. We're getting bitten by mosquitos anyway."

With no moves left and no ideas forthcoming from us, Izzy deflated like a balloon. He stopped dancing and stood still, gasping to catch his breath. As we began to wriggle backwards out of the hedge, Izzy gave it one last valiant shot, and bellowed his favourite movie lines at Pappu.

"Keep the change, ya filthy animal. If I can change, and you can change, everybody can change. *Rishte mein to hum tumhare baap hote hai – naam hai Shahenshah.*"

And with these parting shots from *Home Alone*, *Rocky IV*, and *Shahenshah*, the fearsome Egyptian Mummy turned and fled.

CHAPTER SEVENTEEN

Hairy Tales

In the movies of the 80s and 90s, especially in Bollywood, children were depicted as little angels. They wore frilly frocks and shorts, had curly hair and rosy cheeks, and spoke in cloyingly sweet voices. Every time one of them appeared onscreen, Aji looked at us and grumbled, "Look at that! See how politely she's talking. Why can't you be like that?"

The four of us would look at each other, roll our eyes, and make the loud vomiting sounds that Aji hated. We always had scratches on our forearms and scabs on our knees. There was mud under our nails from making mud pies, sticky sweets melting in the pockets of our uniforms, and half-eaten apples mouldering in our school bags. But we thought we were perfect and didn't see any room for improvement.

Kuku and Ritu, being the youngest, were under the most pressure to be adorable. People looked at their soft eyes and silky hair and assumed they would be docile and gentle. They often received presents of frilly frocks, white lace socks, flowery hairbands, and ribbons for their ponytails.

But instead of walking sedately and holding hands like sweet little girls, Kuku and Ritu tussled their way through the house, banging heads on walls and pinching each other till they screamed.

A few minutes later, they were huddled in a corner with their heads together, whispering secrets and making god-promises not to tell anyone.

But of all the horrible things about us that Aji might have wanted to change, the biggest one was our propensity to pick up lice. Out of the four of us, it was inevitable that someone brought home lice from school every month.

De-lousing us was a regular weekend task for Aji and it involved hours of effort: Four baths with Mediker shampoo, each bath time to be refereed because it often turned into a water fight, and then sitting in the sun and combing four heads with a special comb, examining our scalps while we wriggled and fidgeted. But Aji said anything was better than watching her grandchildren scrape at their heads with pencils and spoons, just like monkeys.

To keep the problem under control, the four of us had to suffer regular haircuts. Daddy bundled us into the car once a month and took us to Balu's Barber Shop when we needed a trim. Balu had only two hair styles in his repertoire: one that was inspired by Amitabh Bachhan, and one that made our faces look like square TV screens. Of course, Daddy got the Amitabh version, while we came out with heads that looked like four Onida TVs in decreasing size.

Balu's shop was in the middle of the city, and he ran a tight ship. He had four swivelling chairs and no assistant apart from a small boy who swept and ran errands. There were often four customers in the seats, looking just like shuttlecocks with their smooth wet heads and flaring plastic sheets wrapped tightly at the neck. Balu floated between the chairs, cutting a sideburn here and covering a bald patch there until he completed all the haircuts in one go.

The four of us had long decided we didn't like Balu. When we arrived at his shop, he dusted off a long bench for us to wait on, sent his assistant scurrying for a thimble-sized cup of tea for Daddy, and kept up a running stream of chatter to entertain us. He liked to joke about cutting our ears off by mistake, and all the other customers thought he was very funny. We sat there sulkily, the butt of all the jokes in a tiny salon, waiting to be made ugly by Balu's scissor-wielding skills while Daddy caught up on the cricket score.

When it was our turn, Balu placed a plank across the bars of his chair so we could sit high enough for him to work on our heads.

After smartly snapping a plastic sheet and throwing it around us with a flourish, he'd douse our heads with water, comb our hair straight down over our faces, and then cut a square window in front so we could see the world and eat our meals. Sometimes the fringe was at eyebrow level, and sometimes we came back with the fringe high up near our hairline, and he always blamed us for moving our heads at the last minute.

It's not possible that Daddy and Aji were blind to how ridiculous we looked, or that they didn't mind seeing their precious treasures being turned into TV screens. But once Daddy had found a suitable barber, there was no way we were going to change, so we would just have to get used to it. In the meantime, we scraped our short fringes back with hairbands, slicked our heads with water or coconut oil, and braved the mockery at school for a week or two until it grew back.

But Balu's masterpieces were not the worst haircuts we've had. It was when we decide to take matters into our own hands that we truly began to look like ugly gnomes.

Ritu came home from Balu once with a terrible haircut. We had convinced her that she'd look like Princess Diana with a short, boyish style, and Balu promised he understood what we meant. She came back looking like Prince Charles instead, and we laughed all the way back. Izzy even offered to get her a paper bag so she could cover her head. We only stopped when Ritu's face crumpled and hot tears rolled down her face.

Daddy left us to take our baths, with strict instructions to wash our hair properly so we wouldn't get barber's rash. Ritu was still crying, and out of guilt and desperation, I suggested that if we shaved her initials in the back of her head, it would look cool instead of ugly. She paused for a few seconds to consider this, and we took immediate action.

Whisking our sniffling Prince Charles lookalike onto a chair in front of the mirror, Kuku wrapped a towel around her neck, and Izzy went rummaging through Daddy's razors for the sharpest one. Kuku lathered the back of Ritu's head with Lifebuoy. Then Izzy and Kuku mouth-breathed behind me while I carefully shaved Ritu's initials into her hair.

We washed off the lather and patted it dry, eagerly assuring her that she would be the talk of the school. Ritu peered at us in the mirror as we examined it, her lip still trembling and her eyes anxious.

For once in our lives, we were at a loss for words. No matter how you looked at, no matter how you leaned your head this way and that, you couldn't tell that there were initials shaved into her hair. A pale and uneven patch went all the way up the back of her head, and there was no chance of ever hiding that.

Storms of tears and recriminations followed, and Daddy and Aji had difficulty keeping a straight face. Ritu was allowed to stay home from school the next day, but it took weeks to grow back.

CHAPTER EIGHTEEN

Kannada Sir

When we were in school, we had to endure short tests every two months, and big exams in October and in March. While each of us had our own favourite subjects and some that we were good at, we were usually too busy to study. The castle we were building from cardboard boxes, the squirrel baby that we were nursing in a shoe box, the latest set of puppies to be looked after, the delightfully tart amlas that had just appeared in our old tree – these were the things that occupied us.

This meant that every two months, we brought home report cards that burned holes in our school bags. The school gave us two days to get our parents to sign the reports, and for those two days, the report cards hung over our heads like an axe.

We woke up and looked drearily at each other, knowing we would have to show them to Daddy soon. In school, we compared strategies with friends about how to get the signatures. At night, we whispered to each other in the dark, telling ourselves we would do it tomorrow.

Despite our strategies, all the kids we knew had only one way for getting signatures. We never gave our parents too much time to look at our appalling report cards, hoping that the red 'F for fail' marks wouldn't be seared onto their minds.

Before we left for school, while Daddy was jangling the car keys and yelling at us to hurry up and stop messing about, we'd line up sheepishly and pull out our report cards. Daddy would look at us with a big sigh and then take up the reports one by one. Cold sweat dripped down our spines as his eyes flicked over the marks. Eclipse slipped away into the far corners of the house, abandoning us to our fate.

When it came, the storm of recrimination was a relief. The first outburst was always the most dramatic, but then we knew we were over the worst part of the ordeal. After that, we got long lectures on the way to and from school, and had to appear serious about our study time for a few days.

Study time was supervised by Aji, and although she reprimanded us once in a while, the four of us loved nothing more than to sit and chat with her about what we had done that day. We sat around her on small footstools, our study books dangling uselessly in our hands while we jumped up to enact a scene from school. Study time melted into dinner time and we always promised Aji that we would study tomorrow.

Daddy knew this and he knew Aji enjoyed these evenings as much as we did. While he believed that having a childhood and spending time with our grandmother was more important than mugging up history, he also worried about our academic futures.

Kannada was our nemesis. We had no aptitude at all and very little interest. Aji learned more Kannada than we did, helping us revise over and over until she knew it and was sure we knew it too. But the next day, we'd stare at the page as if we'd never seen it before.

The Kannada syllabus had grown harder over the years and even Kannada-speaking families were having trouble with it. But to be fair, the four of us spent more time giggling at each other's wisecracks during study time than studying.

After one particularly horrifying report card display, in which all four of the young Khots failed miserably, Daddy and Aji decided it was time to bring in the big guns. They made some phone calls and talked to other parents, and finally found a tutor for us. And so Kannada Sir came into our lives.

Kannada Sir had retired now, but he had been a respected Kannada journalist in his time and had taught in many colleges. Although he wasn't used to teaching kids, he must have assumed it wouldn't be too different from teaching teenagers. He wasn't above smacking us on the head if we chattered with each other, slouched in our seats, or laughed at our own mistakes. The hour we spent with him was the most disciplined hour of our day.

Everyone in our bungalow compound, from Aji and Daddy to the families in the outhouse knew that he was the last hope for the Khot kids. They called him Kannada Sir and treated him with appropriate deference and respect. The coconut trees parted for him when he cycled through our gate, angels trumpeted in heaven when he parked in the porch, and the dogs shivered and cowered as he creakily bent to take off his trouser clips from his legs.

He only had time for us very early in the morning, so everyone made a big push to change their routines to accommodate him. Aji and Daddy set their alarms an hour early so that they could boot us out of bed and force us through brushing our teeth and washing our faces. Kanappa and Tulsi Bai set their alarms so that they could roll open the gate, sweep the verandah where our class took place, and make tea for Kannada Sir.

Five minutes before 6 am, whether it was still dark and misty in winter, or grey and pouring in the monsoon, or bright and warm in summer, Kannada Sir cycled slowly up to the porch and parked his cycle. He liked us to be at the table when he sat down, with our books lined up in front of us, open to fresh blank pages, with our pencils poised and ready. And so the entire household conspired to make sure we were seated according to his directions.

At 5:30 in the morning, the four of us, still sleepy and with pillow creases on our cheeks, sat around Aji and morosely dipped bread in our mugs of tea. We listened grumpily while Aji recited her daily instructions to us to pay attention, write neatly, commit everything to memory, and be grateful that a great educator like Kannada Sir had deigned to teach us.

Kanappa kept watch at the dark corner behind our house, and came running in to announce Kannada Sir had been spotted on the road. That was our cue to jerk into action. We grabbed our books and ran to the table, dragging Kuku if she wasn't ready, or pulling sweaters over Ritu's head while we ran, just in time to slam our bums into the chair as he turned into the gate.

Tulsi Bai would start rattling around in the kitchen to prepare the tray for Kannada Sir, which had to be just so. He was served in our 'special occasion' cutlery, and it was always the same: a glass of water and two biscuits on a saucer. If Tulsi Bai ever put three biscuits on the saucer, he offered it to us or left it untouched.

He drank his tea noisily, crunched his biscuits with enjoyment, and washed it all down with a sip of water. Then he flicked out a snowy handkerchief from his pocket, patted the corners of his mouth, rubbed his whole face down, smoothed his bushy grey eyebrows, blew his nose, and cleaned the corners of his eyes. We always stopped our reading to watch, fascinated by the ritual, until he emerged from his handkerchief with a grunt that meant our class could begin.

Izzy and Kuku got regular smacks from Kannada Sir, but Ritu and I managed to do well enough to get through class without any violence. He made up nicknames for two of us – Carrot Girl for Ritu and Apple Face Boy for Izzy. These must have been popular nicknames in Kannada, but we never understood it.

That year, Kannada Sir made the mistake of accepting Daddy's casual invitation to the Holi party we were having. We didn't expect him, with his white handkerchief and precise ways, to be a Holi player, so we weren't worried that he would show up.

On Holi morning, kids from bungalows all around Fort wandered the roads like marauding thieves, entering the gardens of strangers to collect food or sweets or to participate in a fierce water balloon fight. Hindi movie songs played at full volume from every bungalow, grown-ups got beer by mid-morning and the kids guzzled sugary drinks until they were jittery and twitching.

We woke up early so we could get a head start on the day. Aji rubbed our arms and necks with coconut oil, gripping our heads tight so she could daub oil in our ears and nostrils, in the vain hope that the colour would wash off easily later. We squirmed and complained, and shot out of her hands as soon as she loosened her grip, so we could go and check our arrangements.

In the days leading up to Holi, we spent hours in the chikoo tree, watching as Daddy carefully rigged up a bucket with a pull-rope on the outermost branches so we could overturn water onto people's heads. We shrieked as Kanappa stood on the edge of our pool, reached in with a stick and batted the frogs out all over the garden, just like Kapil Dev hitting sixers. Then we jumped in, sliding on the algae to scrub it out while he hosed it down. We filled it and waited for Holi morning so we could throw people in and jump in ourselves.

When Kannada Sir arrived on that fateful Holi morning, we had already overdosed on sugar and adrenaline. Zayra, Aaliya, and Pinky were there, and we were engaged in an all-out war with the kids from another bungalow in the backyard.

Kuku had a *pichkari* aimed at the kids opposite. Ritu fought beside her, looking oddly misshapen with all the water balloons stuffed inside her shirt and in the pockets of her shorts. Having broken the pull-rope in his excitement, Izzy had now climbed up the chikoo tree and was inching towards the bucket, ready to send down God's own deluge onto our unlucky opponents.

But then Kannada Sir cycled up and parked calmly under the chikoo tree. All of us froze when we saw him, straightening our spines automatically. Two streaks of blue marked his cheeks where someone had respectfully patted him with colour. His shirt was pristine white and his eyebrows unruffled.

For a few seconds, there was silence, except for the speakers that pumped out catchy Bollywood Holi songs. Kannada Sir smiled at us in a sporting manner and fumbled in his pocket for a packet of colour. We had a lot of pent-up anger against him for the morning smacks, especially Kuku and Izzy, and Holi was a great leveller. We eyed him speculatively, weighing the pros and cons of an attack.

Apparently Izzy saw only pros, because as Kannada Sir pinched a few grams of colour out with careful fingers, Izzy let out a banshee howl from the tree. Some kind of primal thrill ran through all the kids – there must have been about twelve of us – and we banded together in unity against the evil tuition teacher.

Izzy overturned the bucket, sending a waterfall down on Kannada Sir's head from fifteen feet high. In his enthusiasm, the heavy steel bucket slipped from Izzy's hands, whizzing past within inches of our educator's venerable head.

The bucket was followed by Izzy, who dropped to the ground, bounded up like a miniature ape, and jumped onto Kannada Sir's chest, holding his arms down and shouting "Get him, get him" at us.

We leapt into action, unleashing a barrage of Holi hell on him. Those who had *pichkaris* squirted him right in the face, aiming for the eyes. Those who didn't have *pichkaris* flung water with a mug, and someone lobbed the mug too.

Kannada Sir staggered in circles, trying to get loose from the boy who stuck to him like a leech. We screamed and danced, and then someone shrieked "Pool, pool!" and we whooped in agreement.

Kanappa emerged from the sanctuary of his room just in time to see twelve kids tackling a grown man to the ground. It took a few seconds but Kanappa blanched in horror when he realised what we were about to do, and to whom. Kannada Sir wasn't a tall man, and we wrapped our scrawny arms around his legs, head, arms, and feet, so that we could half-carry and half-drag him around the side of the bungalow.

Kanappa ran after us, shouting at us to stop, but we were already in too deep and didn't look back. He shouted for help, calling to the grown-ups to stop us, but everyone was already in the pool, laughing and chatting as they bobbed in the water. The music system blasted the best of Bollywood Holi songs, and nobody heard Kanappa's warning.

A human centipede with a body made of Kannada Sir and twenty-four fast-pumping legs approached the pool at full speed. Kannada Sir shouted unholy swearwords and tried to struggle free, but the small fingers clung tighter and the short legs ran even faster.

The kids who had wandered in from the other bungalow didn't even know who he was, but in a battle between kids and adults, they knew whose side they were on. We clambered up onto the rim of the pool with our treasure and plunged straight into the water.

Daddy and a few other grown-ups turned to see what made the big splash and saw Kannada Sir coming up for air. Twelve pairs of hands pushed his head under again while the grown-ups stared in disbelief. All those years of cycling had given Kannada Sir strong legs and it took all our strength to remain in place while he lashed kicks out at us, but we remained doggedly in position, with some of us holding our breath and staying underwater if needed.

Kanappa ran up puffing and shouting, and broke the shocked spell that Daddy was under. He sprang into action, lunging over to pluck us off one by one and fling us back into the water. Kannada Sir emerged spluttering and choking as Daddy thumped him on the back. Kanappa didn't know what to do so he leaned over the edge of the pool and offered a glass of water. Kannada Sir spat water out and looked at Kanappa sharply, but realised he was only trying to be hospitable.

We cowered by the sides of the pool. Whatever demons had possessed us had now vanished into thin air and we were suddenly aware of the terrible crime we had committed and the punishment that awaited us. Would we be put into vats of boiling oil? Would we be hung from trees so the crows could pluck out our eyeballs? Would we be fed to the sharks?

The kids from the other bungalow melted away in the direction of the gate, never to be seen again, and we wished we could do the same. Kannada Sir reached into a pocket and took out a dripping wet handkerchief to wipe his face, before facing us. We held our breath.

"Good trick, Apple Face Boy! Good trick. Happy Holi!"

CHAPTER NINETEEN

Ghost Stories

Looking back now, it seemed like the clocks in Belgaum ticked at a different pace. Parents dawdled outside the school gates to chat with other parents. The teachers in our school enjoyed comfortable cups of tea with each other between classes. If you walked into a store in the market, the owner always made time to put their elbows on the counter and indulge in a few minutes of conversation. Everyone knew each other and made time to stop and ask how you were doing.

This was also the perfect environment for ghost stories to spread like wildfire. Gullible kids in school lapped up news of supernatural events and repeated them at dinner tables across Belgaum that night. Maids and drivers passed on the scariest stories to their employers, who immediately picked up the phone to relay the news. Everyone had time to talk and the best social currency was a good ghost story. The four of us were just as susceptible, and were always ready to drop everything and listen with wide eyes and open mouths.

Belgaum had its share of women in white saris hitching bike rides on the lonely roads near the Belgaum Club, only to disappear from the pillion seat mid-ride. We heard of babies born with snake skin because their father had killed a snake once. We even had a dismembered hand in our school toilets, which terrorised everyone for the whole day and made some girls cry, until an ayah smacked them and showed us it was just a rubber cleaning glove with iodine on it.

But these were stories that died down in a few days. Only one legend swept Belgaum and lasted for weeks: *Naale Ba*, the old lady with the hunchback, who came to take away the youngest child in the house.

Naale Ba means *Come Tomorrow* in Kannada. According to the legend, if you wrote *Naale Ba* on your door with chalk, she'd read it and go away, promising to come back again. The next day, she'd see it again and leave, so that the littlest members of your house were safe.

Now our verandah was enclosed by an iron grill, so we didn't actually have a front door, but we had to do something to protect Kuku. She depended on us for her life. The four of us held an emergency meeting after school that day, and Kuku sat beside us, twisting her hands nervously and awaiting our decision with big scared eyes. None of us knew what the old hunchback did with the little children she collected, but we were sure it meant a terrible fate for Kuku.

We decided to make a sign to put up on the grill, but Ritu warned us that might not be enough.

"She'll have to walk all the way in through our gate and up the driveway to see the sign," Ritu pointed out. "What if she sees Eclipse in the garden and takes him instead? He's younger than Kuku."

She had a good point. We decided we couldn't take that risk, and so we upturned our box of coloured chalk pieces and set to work. Daddy was out that evening, but when he drove up to the verandah, he noticed that we had scrawled the spell on the driveway leading up to our house, as well as on the walls of our house, the trunks of trees, the cycles, the scooter, the sides of the pool, and the lovebird cage.

He'd heard about the old lady but he hadn't expected his children to lose their heads. When he strode into our study room to ask what the hell we were up to, all of us turned from our desks to look at him.

Daddy opened his mouth to begin his lecture about blindly believing everything we heard, and then he saw it – the bold-lettered *Naale Ba* sign made from notebook paper, heavily underlined and coloured in red, pinned to the front of Kuku's dress.

He looked at her oddly, took in our strained faces and chalk-stained clothes, and seemed to choke on something. He closed the door carefully and went back out, and we heard him and Aji chuckling about it. We looked darkly at each other over our study books. They might not care about Kuku, but we had done what we had to do to protect her.

But although we banded together to defeat the threat of *Naale Ba*, it was the story of Chandni that really captured our imaginations. I first heard about Chandni in school and repeated it at bedtime for Izzy and the smallies.

"Hundreds of years ago in Belgaum, there lived a beautiful girl. This story is not about her life, but about her ghastly end."

Kuku and Ritu sighed happily and settled back into their pillows, while Izzy propped his chin on his hands in the top bunk and listened.

"She was a dancer in the royal court, and she moved with the grace of a moonbeam, delighting the king and queen. They named her Chandni and declared that she would wear only white silk outfits with silver anklets that tinkled when she walked. Everyone admired her for her beauty and her pure nature, but Chandni fell in love with a handsome man with a black heart. He promised for many months to marry her, but when she asked him to buy her wedding bangles, he got angry and pushed her over a cliff to her death. When Chandni's ghost came back for revenge, she wasn't beautiful any longer. Her face was covered in blood and she had to hold her broken head together. Even today, she walks about on dark nights, jingling her anklets and looking for revenge on all men."

All of us shivered deliciously and sympathized with poor Chandni, and then turned over to go to sleep. We had forgotten about Chandni by the next morning, but a few days later we realised how useful she was going to be to us.

The smallies and I were cleaning our cupboards out when we found an old pair of anklets from last Diwali. It's amazing how one idea can cross three minds at the same time. We looked at each other and smirked.

The three of us had a score to settle with Izzy. He had recently moved his desk to a separate room, claiming that we were chattering too much and distracting him from studying. Daddy gave the three of us a lecture about how we should help each other instead of hindering each other's growth, and made us help move Izzy's books. All the while, Izzy stood behind Daddy with a virtuous look on his face. We knew Izzy just wanted to read his comic books till late in the night, but we held our tongues and swore revenge.

That night, after we'd finished our baths and dinner, Aji went off to watch her TV programmes and Izzy disappeared into his room. The three of us checked to make sure Daddy was busy with the newspapers and then slipped out through the back door, bundling the anklets tightly in our nighties so they wouldn't jingle until we were ready.

Anyone who has ever owned a dog knows that they have their own unique set of sounds. While we lay in our beds, we could hear their claws clattering on the ground outside the window as they chased shadows. We could hear their ears flapping against their skull every time they shook their heads to wake up. We could hear them grunting or huffing when they ran, or barking to each other all night.

These noises were a part of our lives and we barely noticed them, but there was always a rhythm to them. But on those quiet nights inside the Fort, our noisy dogs could give us away within seconds. If he heard noises that were out of the ordinary, Izzy would know that something was up.

While Ritu and I carried the anklets and the flashlight, we gave Kuku the task of keeping the dogs quiet. Although they had spent the whole evening bowling along by our sides on our way to tuition classes, Rum and Raisin suffered intense grief when we went indoors for the night. If we appeared outside the house after dark, they assumed that it was a special occasion and were determined to mark it with the appropriate celebrations. They whined and squeaked, barked and clattered their claws, but eventually were calmed by Kuku's small patting hands.

We padded soundlessly around to Izzy's window, communicating with gestures and whispers. He had pushed the desk up to face the window, and we crept close and peered in. The room was dark but Izzy sat at his table, illuminated by the small pool of light that his table lamp made. To his credit, he was actually studying.

Ritu unwrapped the anklets carefully and handed them over. I held them up and gave one gentle tinkle. Izzy looked up and around. He had a peculiar way of sliding his ears backwards when he was startled or scared, so we knew exactly when the thought of Chandni crossed his mind. He looked fearfully over his shoulder into the dark room, then straightened his back, shook his head, probably invoked Rambo, and turned to his books again.

We were right outside his window, so close that we could have reached out and smacked him if the mosquito mesh hadn't been between us. But because he sat in the light and we were in the dark, he couldn't see us at all.

We waited a few minutes until he persuaded himself that he had imagined it. Just as he began to feel safe, we jingled the anklet again. Izzy flinched. His pencil stopped moving and he lifted his head, but kept his eyes trained on his desk, too scared to look up at the dark window in case the bloodthirsty Chandni stood there, holding her head together.

The three of us held our hands to our mouths to hold back the laughter, but the sight of Izzy glued to his seat, immobile with fear at the mature age of 9 years was too much for us and we were choking. When we couldn't manage that any longer, I gave up and shook the anklet about wildly, creating an unnatural jingling. Izzy leapt up, sending his chair skidding backwards and charged out, away from the lonely room and the dark window, followed by our shrieks of laughter.

The next day he moved his desk back into our room, and we were reunited again.

CHAPTER TWENTY

The Terrible Injection Story

The four of us were fairly brave for kids. We were the grandchildren of GW Khot, who was the first Indian to become Deputy Inspector General of the Indian Police. He had killed man-eating tigers that were terrorizing villages. He led a campaign to end the reign of Man Singh, the most blood-thirsty dacoit that India had ever seen. We asked for these stories over and over, and knew that nothing less than pure courage was expected from us.

Much of our bravery came from Daddy's blithe certainty that we would be okay. When we went out on weekend treks, he tied ropes around us and lowered us into crevasses over waterfalls. With his rallying encouragement, we went swimming in the unknown green waters of reservoirs, hiked through forests where leopards and wild boar were frequently spotted, and camped in parks with knives under our pillows in case a black bear showed up at night.

But our iron-willed lineage failed us when it came to injections. No amount of inspirational stories could bolster our wavering courage when the time came to be vaccinated. Apart from regular vaccinations, we were also frequently injuring ourselves on rusty nails or getting bitten or scratched by stray animals, requiring shots for rabies or tetanus.

Uncle Zaheer was a familiar figure to us, partly because we spent so much time at Zayra and Aaliya's house, and partly because he had cured every stomach ache, flu, and fever in our house. Aji had asthma and frequent joint pain, and he often visited to check on her and share a cup of tea and a comfortable chat.

When Uncle Zaheer visited Aji, we didn't mind stopping our games to show him a wobbling tooth or to let him check how that old wound was healing.

But there were some days when the atmosphere seemed charged with a different kind of energy. If Uncle Zaheer avoided meeting our eye and rummaged in his bag while Daddy and Kanappa converged upon us, we knew it was injection time again.

Nobody ever warned us about this, but we sensed it. Within seconds, the four of us took off in different directions, running as fast as our short legs could carry us, melting into the shadows of the garden to disappear for hours.

Kanappa and Daddy, having learned from bitter experience, jumped into our paths, arms outstretched and feet planted wide like football goalkeepers. If we were nimble enough, we could dodge under a hand and escape for a while, but eventually each of us was carried in, kicking and screaming.

Uncle Zaheer always had the syringe and the cotton swab prepped, and would grab whichever arm or buttock he could and jab the injection in. After that, the mortally wounded victim was passed on, wailing bitterly, to Aji to be petted and soothed, and Daddy and Kanappa would set off for the next one. It was an exhausting and traumatic event for everyone, and I often wonder how Uncle Zaheer had the patience to deal with us.

The next day, the four of us were usually kept at home because we had developed fever as a reaction to the medicine. Sullen and indignant, refusing to talk to Daddy and Kanappa, we lay wrapped in blankets in front of the television, the only day of the year when we were allowed to watch Disney movies during the day, nursing our sore arms or buttocks with a martyred air.

After all that fuss, if we needed any additional injections because of an injury we had brought upon ourselves, we bore it stoically. We knew that if we caught an arm on a rusty nail, tetanus shots were in order. We still had to be chased and caught, but we didn't thrash like fish on hooks to get away.

One day, a team of workers had been called in to clear the overgrown grass in our garden. The four of us floated about between them, falling upon long-lost cricket balls and forgotten boomerangs with cries of joy. Daddy shouted at me a couple of times to get back in the house and put my shoes on before a snake got me, but I was just far enough away from him to ignore his warning.

Izzy and I were running at full speed, rejoicing in the scent of fresh greenery when something sharp stabbed my foot. I fell over and clutched my leg, terrified that I'd actually been bitten by a snake. It took a few seconds to understand what had happened. I had stepped on some sort of skull and shattered it, and pieces of bone lay shattered around my foot. One shard had driven deep into the soft flesh of my sole, and Izzy skidded up just in time to see blood beginning to spurt like a fountain out of my foot.

He opened his mouth once or twice, then turned and ran straight to Daddy. I waited there for Daddy to come and pick me up, dully watching blood splatter onto my leg and on the ground around me.

Through the fog of shock, it suddenly occurred to me that this was an animal skull, and that meant I would need 12 rabies shots. Twelve injections. I couldn't even comprehend the horror of that, and I started mumbling *No No No* to myself.

By the time Daddy rushed over, I had disappeared. He saw the blood and the skull, and then sent everyone to look for me. It didn't take long because even though I had hopped on my good foot, I had left a bloody trail. I was discovered hiding deep under a table in the darkest room of the house.

Kuku and Ritu tried to drag me out, but I let out such a loud and frightening howl that they let me go quickly.

Izzy, who would have loved a tug-of-war challenge like this at any other time, was strangely quiet. Izzy and I were close to each other, and under his boisterous nature, he had the softest heart of all four of us. He ran off to get cotton wool and Dettol. More than anyone else in the house, Izzy knew the drill for injuries.

Daddy arrived and bent down beside the table. In all our lives, Daddy has never baby-talked us, even when we were babies. We were treated like individual (albeit small-sized) people who could make the right choice when presented with the truth. If he told us not to do something, he always explained to us why he was saying so. Of course, if we carried on doing it, we got the warm side of his hand, which was a big and heavy hand.

"Mahi, you know we have to clean your wound immediately, don't you? You have to come out now."

"No!" I shrank back into the darkness, pulling my foot towards me.

"Baby, do you know what it was that you stepped on?"

"A thorn?" I knew exactly what it was and I knew what came next. I was just trying my luck.

"No, my pet. That was a cat skull. Some stray cat must have died there, and you stepped on the lower jaw bone. The cat's tooth has pierced your flesh."

I started crying again. "But I don't want to get 12 injections."

"No, no. I don't think you'll have to get injections." Daddy knew exactly what it was and he knew what came next, but he was just trying to get me out from under the table. "But we have to clean your wound and see how deep it is."

I was immediately consoled and began to crawl out. "Okay, but don't touch it."

Daddy took me into the bathroom and held my foot under running tap water, dousing it liberally with Dettol. After that, I was laid out on the table and Daddy, along with his team of crack surgeons – Kuku, Ritu, and Izzy – peered at my foot.

They rolled my foot about for a few seconds, and then Daddy leapt up and stalked off, shooting over his shoulder to us that he had to make a few phone calls. Izzy was asked to press a wad of cotton wool to the bleeding hole in my foot, while Kuku and Ritu described to me how deep they could see into my flesh.

Then Daddy came back, batted away the smallies and Izzy, and bundled me into the Sumo. I was driven to Praful Kaka's hospital and carried straight into his cabin. Praful Kaka was Daddy's cousin and my uncle, and I liked him. He had a big twirling moustache and a big belly and a big jolly laugh. He drove about Belgaum at full speed in a green Jeep, and always had a couple of dogs fawning around his legs.

In the waiting room of the hospital, Praful Kaka delivered the news to me that I'd have to get twelve injections. I started bawling again, painfully aware this time that I was in a strange place with nowhere to run, without the support of Izzy and Ritu and Kuku.

Then Daddy told me the story of what happened to people who got rabies. "They have to be tied up, baby, and although they're begging for water, if you give them a glass, they go pale and start shouting 'take it away, take it away from me' as if it's going to poison them."

"Hydrophobia," Praful Kaka nodded. "It's very sad to see it. They froth at the mouth, and they don't recognise their own family, the people that they love."

Praful Kaka showed me a pamphlet from his drawer, with a horrible snarling dog on the front, where it said some of the things they had just told me, albeit with less drama. It was time to accept my fate. I knew I had to get the first injection on Day 0, and there was no way I was escaping this.

Praful Kaka busied himself with the tray and Daddy turned my face away to the other side. He asked me if we should buy ice cream on the way back and surprise the smallies. While we were discussing which flavour we should choose, Praful Kaka gave me the first injection.

I discovered that although he was so big, he had the lightest touch. I barely felt the injection and within a few seconds, he was pressing a ball of cotton wool into my arm and smiling down at me. Maybe it won't be so bad, I thought to myself.

But while I was beginning to get used to the idea of multiple injections in the near future, Daddy was worrying. We'd be leaving for our summer holiday before I finished my course of twelve injections, and there was no doctor to administer the last one.

For our summer holidays, we were visiting Grandpa in London. We'd be arriving in London during Easter weekend, on the day that I was supposed to take the last one. There was no time to arrange the insurance and paperwork, or get a private appointments that weekend.

There was no other option. By the time I was getting my fifth injection, Praful Kaka was training Daddy to give me my last shot.

On the day of my last shot, we were in London. Jet-lagged and exhausted from the flight and the long drive to my grandfather's house, I was barely able to stay awake. We had carried the last vial of Rabipur vaccine in a flask filled with ice, and there were five syringes lined up on the table – four for practice and one for me.

Grandpa sat at the table in his vest, alternating between delivering pep talks to me and to Daddy. A slice of defrosted steak lay on a plate in front of us. Daddy was practising on it with the spare syringes filled with water.

From our vast medical knowledge, gained from *Baywatch* and *Doogie Howser*, we knew that if Daddy let a bubble of air go into my veins, I would die.

I had never seen Daddy nervous before, but today he was strangely pale under his beard. I sat close to the steak, with my sleeve rolled up and a dot marked on my arm where the injection was to go. I watched Daddy's long fingers pick up the practice syringe.

The walls of the room seemed to close in on me and the air felt thick and warm. I longed for a cool breeze or a splash of water on my face. The latest shot of water swelled under the skin of the steak, making the pink meat wobble. My own stomach wobbled, and I swallowed and looked at Daddy.

Daddy nodded at Izzy to swab my arm with antiseptic. Grandpa pinched my chin and twisted my face away so I wouldn't look. I looked into my grandfather's eyes and he smiled encouragingly. Kuku and Ritu slipped their rough little hands into mine.

It was over in a few seconds and I turned back to face everyone. Five pairs of eyes watched anxiously, trying to calculate how long it would take for any oxygen bubbles to make their way to my heart. I waited too until Daddy declared that this was morbid and I was fine. I took a deep breath and smiled shakily.

"Oh, that's excellent!" shouted Grandpa, grabbing Daddy's hand and pumping it up and down. "Well done! Well done! Ice-cream for all!"

Then he slumped forward onto the table and fainted gracefully.

CHAPTER TWENTY ONE

Fireflies in Jars

In our world, life revolved around our school calendar. As we returned from the summer vacation, we plunged straight into the new school year. We reluctantly put aside our holiday memories and began to leaf through the syllabus for the coming year. Izzy and I looked over the shoulders of the smallies at their hand-me-down text books, nodded sagely and warned them about the chapters that we had already struggled with in the previous years.

The first week was a frenzy of trying on new uniforms and buying stiff shoes that would bite our tender toes for weeks. At night, Aji and Daddy worked feverishly to cover our notebooks with brown paper, as the school had instructed. The four of us sharpened pencils, packed our school bags, and filled fountain pens with ink, squabbling over whose turn it was to take the complete geometry set, and who would have to make do with the cracked protractor.

But as the new school year began, the monsoon intensified around us. Our classrooms smelled damp and musty, and so did our classmates. We sat through classes in wet, itchy socks with mud splattering the backs of our legs.

Coughs and colds raged through the school, and in a house with four children, we took turns to fall ill. Aji dosed us on *haldi* milk, rubbed our chests and foreheads with Vicks Vaporub until our eyes watered, and put us to bed with hot water bottles.

One weekend, Daddy was striding through the house, mid-way through some project of his own design, when he stumbled upon the four of us in the guest bedroom. This was our favourite spot. Tucked away on the side of the house, this was the least visited room, so we were unlikely to be interrupted by the grown-ups. It had two large cupboards filled with books and old clothes, so we could read and play dress-up all day long.

Today however, Izzy and I were recovering from a viral flu and were lying languidly in bed, feeling sorry for ourselves. Aji had tried to separate us when one was ill so we wouldn't pass on the germs, but we always found our way to where the sniffling fourth of our team was. This worked against us when I brought home chicken pox and immediately infected the others. But Uncle Zaheer, with his unique understanding of all of us, assured Aji that we made each other feel better and were cranky when apart, so it was best not to enforce any separation.

When we were ill, we enjoyed special treatment. I could lie in bed and read all day, without being reminded to do my homework. Izzy could ask for hot Bournvita and sandwiches at any time of the day, and nobody brushed him off or told him that his stomach was a bottomless pit. Both of us could boss the smallies around to fetch things for us, and they couldn't protest much.

And so, even though we had already recovered from our flu, we were milking this opportunity for all it was worth. Cosily ensconced in a nest of blankets and pillows and a cat, Izzy and I had dragged our blankets up to our noses and were watching Kuku and Ritu having a kicking fight. This involved drawing one's knee up as far as one could and unleashing a string of rapid kicks on the other, with Izzy calling out the score.

"That's not even a proper kick, Kuku. You have to land on the shin at least" Izzy rasped, struggling to sit up. "Don't expect me to give you any points for…."

He broke off when Daddy entered the room. Daddy didn't get overly upset if we fell out of trees or were scratched when wrestling with our cat or dogs, but if he saw us wilfully inflicting violence on each other, we were in trouble. It was unfortunate that some of our best games involved violence. Kuku and Ritu froze and shoved their legs under my blanket, kneeing me brutally in the stomach.

"What's going on here?" Daddy bellowed. "Why aren't you playing outside? What is this lazy *nawab-sahib* weekend going on?"

"But it's raining, Daddy," Izzy said.

"Nonsense! Put on your raincoat and come outside with me. I need someone to help clean out the junk in the shed."

"But Aji said we should rest, Daddy" I said virtuously. I didn't want to go and clean out the shed, which housed hundreds of disgusting lizards. "We're still recovering from our flu."

Aji came hurrying over from the other room. "No, no!" she protested. "Don't take them out in the rain. I just managed to get Izzy's temperature down yesterday."

"They've recovered, haven't they? And why are all of them rolling about in blankets if only two of them are sick?"

Aji had no answer for this. Neither did we. We just liked each other's company. And besides, what would the smallies do without us to supervise their free time?

"They have to rest, Nitin. I want them to be ready for school tomorrow."

"Tchah! They'll be fine. I'll take them all to school tomorrow. But before that, we're going out to see glow-worms tonight. Pappu told me that the villagers around Yellurgad have been seeing thousands of them for the last week."

"Glow-worms?" Ritu piped up. Ever since the smallies had seen their first firefly, they had called them glow-worms, and now everyone used the same name. Kuku and Ritu were convinced that fireflies were fairy lanterns, and often chased them through the garden.

"Yes! Thousands of them. And it's only for a short while, because once the rains get heavy, the glow-worms will go away." Daddy saw that his four invalids were beginning to perk up. "So are you well enough for that? Or do you want to sit here like lemons all evening?"

Aji and Daddy began a short debate about exposing us to the elements, during which we looked from one to another as shots were volleyed, just like in a tennis match. Finally Daddy stomped off victorious, and Aji walked away, rolling her eyes and grumbling under her breath about trying to keep the kids alive.

We threw our blankets off and hastily began to prepare. We had never gone out to see glow-worms before, but Daddy rattled off some instructions to us and we did as we were told.

We found some old jam jars and rinsed the dust off, then replaced the lids with squares of mosquito net held in place with a rubber band. In a stroke of genius, Izzy grabbed the long-handled net that he used for his fish tank.

Just before dusk, we clambered into the Sumo with our box of jars. Kuku and Ritu laughed as Izzy and I struggled to climb in, encumbered by the layers of warm sweaters and scarves that Aji had forced us to wear. They stopped laughing when Izzy swatted ferociously at them with the long-handle of the net, and peace reigned once more in the back seat.

It was only a short drive from our house, and we were at the village in no time. Daddy exchanged a few words with the villagers to get directions, and we heard them mention leopards. But before we could clarify this, Daddy plunged off into the darkness.

We followed obediently, leaving behind the dim lights of the village and climbing through the forested path that led up the hill.

It was pitch dark, with only the sliver of a new moon in the sky. We could barely make out the shape of the hill in front of us, but we knew it from previous visits.

Daddy was almost jogging up the hill, and we chased after him. Kuku and Ritu pumped their short legs to match his long stride. Izzy was usually the fastest, but today he was struggling with his sweaters and scarves, trying to rip them off as he grew warmer and warmer. He only stopped his fidgeting to tell Kuku how leopards eat their prey.

"You know how they do it?" he whispered, so Daddy wouldn't hear him frightening his youngest sister. "They play with you, like a cat plays with a mouse. They let you run away a bit so you think you're safe, and then they come back and catch you. Then they do it again.

And finally, when they're hungry, they gobble up the most delicious parts first. And they leave some parts for later."

Kuku began to whimper and I punched him so hard that he stopped with a loud *Owwwww*! Daddy turned to look at us and then looked up. We were racing against the clouds which were gathering in a sinister mass overhead.

"Come on, come on! If I let you get caught in the rain, you'll fall ill again tomorrow," Daddy looked at us all as if we were weaklings. "And then Aji will blame me for you all missing school. We'd better get moving. Izzy, stop pulling at your scarf or you'll strangle yourself!"

After a while, Daddy stopped in his tracks. All of us halted where we were, panting heavily.

"What is it, Daddy?" Izzy asked fearfully. "Is it leopards?"

The beams from our flashlights zigzagged wildly around as we spun in circles, expecting to see hordes of bloodthirsty leopards leaping at us from behind each tree. They could probably smell the omelette sandwiches that we'd just eaten.

"What? Leopards? No, that's rubbish! I can't see any fireflies though. I wonder if they've all gone already."

We looked around more calmly this time, but all we could see was darkness. The trees crowded in around us, blocking out even the comforting view of the village lights. We were up here in the middle of nowhere, with leopards pacing about just beyond the trees. Creepy insects clicked and rustled around us and we shuddered and drew closer.

"Daddy, where are the glow-worms? Should we go home if they're not here?" asked Kuku, her knees almost knocking together.

But Daddy didn't answer. We looked around and realised with a shock that he must have headed off into the trees, expecting us to follow him. We were alone in the dark with grown-ups to protect us from the leopards. Ritu uttered a piercing scream and then began to cry gustily. Kuku looked at her and her chin began to tremble.

"No, no. Don't start crying now" exhorted Izzy. "Let's shout for Daddy instead. Daddy! Daddddyyyy!"

The smallies took this up quickly and we banded together in one spot, shouting with all our lung power. "Dadddddyyyyy! Dadddyyyyyy!"

Birds flew up out of the trees, squawking indignantly at us, disturbed from their comfortable roosting by our ear-splitting screams. If there were any leopards watching us from the trees, they must have sprinted away in a hurry too. We stopped to take a breath and opened our mouths again.

"What's wrong with you four?!" Daddy muttered, stumbling through a patch of bushes. "I just went behind the tree for a quick piddle, that's all. You'll bring the villagers up here with all that racket!"

Ritu went up to cuddle Daddy's leg and he patted her head. "Okay, okay, come on now. We're almost there. I'm sure the glow-worms are up there. Let's go check. If they're not, we'll go and buy some ice-cream and go home, alright?"

Mollified, we began the walk up to the top of the hill. This time, the four of us clustered close around Daddy, almost trampling on the backs of his sneakers in our attempt to keep an eye on him. And as it turned out, Daddy was right.

From the ridge on the top of the hill, we could see the glow-worms just below us. It looked as though someone had waved a magic wand and scattered glitter in the air. Tens of thousands of fireflies hovered in mid-air, undulating in waves as they danced to their own rhythm. We watched open-mouthed, until Daddy reminded us that we had jars.

"Just take the net off and walk towards the fireflies slowly, holding it up. You'll catch them inside, and then we can take them back home to show Aji. She'll love these!"

Fascinated by this idea, we ripped the nets off and ran up to the fireflies. Izzy took two jars and charged into the cloud, sending up thousands of glowing bugs into the air, until Daddy shouted to him to calm down.

"Gently! Gently, Izzy. You're not trying to kill them, *baba*. And keep your mouth closed. We don't want to take any home in your mouth."

Kuku and Ritu hopped about, trying to leap into the air to catch more, squealing if one landed on them. We filled six jars and brought them back to Daddy, our palms cupped over the top so he could fit the mosquito net back on top.

Once we had enough to take home to Aji, Daddy showed us how to lie down on the grass and look up at the sky. The clouds were rushing past, but we could see stars beyond them, and glow-worms in the middle. We lay there for a long time on the damp grass, looking up at the stars and the magical glow-worms, smiling to ourselves. Kuku and Ritu held hands and sang *Twinkle Twinkle Little Star* with delight.

The spell was broken when Daddy realised that Izzy had pulled off his sweater and scarf as he lay there. "Oh no! Now you're really going to fall ill. I told you not to take off your sweater when your body is heated up like that. The air is cold outside. Come on now, put them back on."

Izzy struggled back into his warm clothes with some complaints, but Daddy decided it was time to go home. As we drove back, the rain began to fall, first in fat droplets on our windscreen, and then in a thundering deluge. We had descended just in time.

Aji was waiting for us and sent us for our hot baths first, and then followed it up with a piping hot plate of *varan-bhaath*. She praised the glow-worms to us, but made Daddy promise that when he released them later that night, it wouldn't be anywhere inside the house.

Finally it was time for bed. We tucked ourselves in, performed the usual negotiations with Daddy about one last glass of water and one last chance to go to the toilet, before it was *really* time for bed. Daddy brought in the six jars of glow-worms and put them on the dressing table so we could look at them as we fell asleep, and gave us his usual stern warning to stop chattering and close our eyes.

Some memories, no matter how old you get or how far you wander from home, will be imprinted in the very fibres of your soul.

That night, we lay listening to the thunderstorms raging overhead, cosy and cocooned in our tangle of blankets. The *varan-bhaath* made us yawn and feel warm inside. Izzy let out a loud burp from the top bunk and we all giggled sleepily. The glow-worms danced in their jars on the table, looking more and more like enchanted fairy-dust as our eyelids grew heavy and we slipped into a world of star-spangled dreams.

~ The End ~

A Note from the Author

Hello there!

I started writing this book in March 2020, when COVID-19 first shut down our lives. In those early weeks, the reins that we grip so tightly were ripped out of our hands and all we could do was watch in bewilderment as our world descended into chaos.

It felt like the first day of school – all of us scared and unsure, waiting for instructions from someone who knew better. As the days melted into weeks at home, our brains began to rewire the circuitry, pulling up memories and emotions from our childhood to stabilise us and make us feel safe.

We reached out to the ones we love most. We made comfort food that reminded us of the fragrance in our mothers' kitchens. We rediscovered hobbies that we had set aside because they felt childish in our important grown-up lives. We shed ties and suits and stayed in our pyjamas all day, eating pancakes and watching TV.

When a grown-up writes about childhood, it takes some effort to remember what it was like to be two feet tall and not in control of anything. In the last few months, we have been reminded of this in no uncertain way. And although I felt vulnerable and scared, it was also unusually easy to conjure up the unfettered creativity and curiosity of childhood. It turns out that with that loss of control came a strange and uneasy creative freedom.

I began to write my next book, worrying that it wouldn't feel relevant to anyone in the face of our horrible reality. But as I wrote, I was transported to a simpler, sunnier world and the trauma of our daily lives felt less overwhelming.

I wanted this book to be something special, something that distils the strength and bravery we need to get through the pandemic. As I sit here writing this, I know that we're far from done with COVID. But just like the kids in this book, we once knew how to get up and dust ourselves off, and we will learn how to do it all over again.

I'm so glad you read my book. It would be wonderful if you wrote a review for it so that other readers can find these stories too. You can leave a review on Amazon, Goodreads, Kobo, Gumroad, Smashwords, or Google Books. I'll be delighted to see them all.

Big hugs,

Mishana ☺

Acknowledgements

This book was harder for me to edit than my previous books, because the subject is so close to my heart. I prefer doing my own edits for my writing, spreading multiple review sessions out to give myself the distance I need to be objective. In the case of this book, I needed an impartial eye to go over the stories and tell me where I was being redundant or unclear.

Thank you to Rahul, Upamanyu, and Vinoo for reviewing *Welcome to the Zoo*. Your suggestions were perfect, sharp-eyed, and relevant, and while I decided to not implement some, I think you'll find that most of your changes are in the book now, making it so much better.

And lastly, thank you to Amit, my best friend and partner. You're always the first one to read my writing. You're the only one to listen to my angst-ridden debates about characters, plot, and writer's block. You're the one who keeps me stocked up on chocolate, lemongrass tea, chips, and all the other fuel I need to write. You're the one who reminds me to drink enough water, do my stretches, go for a run, and stop writing for long enough to eat something goddammit. Thank you for pushing me to prioritise my writing, and for making me believe I'm the next best thing to happen to readers after Roald Dahl

§

www.mishanakhot.com

All Books by Mishana Khot

A Brave Day for Harold Brown

Merry Christmas, Mr. Brown

Welcome to the Zoo

§

www.mishanakhot.com

Glossary of terms

gulab jamun: Indian dessert made from milk solids, shaped into balls and deep-fried until deep golden brown. After this, they're soaked in sugar syrup that is flavoured with essences of rose and cardamom. These melt-in-your-mouth gulab jamuns are amongst the most popular sweets in India.

baabloo: Term of endearment

beedi: Slender hand-rolled cigarette made by rolling a dried leaf and filling it with tobacco. It does not have a filter and smells quite strong.

tandoor: Traditional oven, originally made with clay and heated by charcoal and wood. The food to be cooked is usually stuck on the sides of the tandoor or placed on skewers inside to cook. As it cooks, juices and fat from the food drips onto the coal below, causing it to smoke and infuse the food with a unique flavour. Anything made inside a tandoor is called tandoori, or 'from a tandoor'.

dargah: A shrine built to mark the grave of a respected religious figure in the Islamic faith.

pao: Soft savoury buns made to be eaten with stews and thick curries.

khichdi: A soft mix of rice and lentils cooked together with very little spice. It is often served to babies, children, and anyone who is not feeling well.

halwa: Rich dessert made with lots of sugar. A variety of vegetables and fruit can be turned into a heavy sweet with the basic recipe.

gadhe ki aulad: The literal meaning is 'son of a donkey'. It is used in a derogatory manner.

raat ki rani: The literal translation is 'Queen of the Night'. This is a species of jasmine plant that blooms at night and has an exquisite fragrance.

idli: Soft round cakes made by steaming rice flour batter. Usually eaten with chutney or sambar. Local to South India.

sambar: A delicious stew made from lentils, soured with tamarind or kokum. Usually also contains seasonal vegetables like carrots, brinjal, pearl onions, moringa drumsticks, and beans.

varan: Mild dal made from lentils with gentle spices like turmeric, asafoetida, and cumin seeds. This dish is considered suitable for babies and children because of the low spice and great digestive benefits. Best when served with steamed rice and ghee.

sabzi: The literal translation is 'vegetables' but it can also be used when talking of main course dishes made with vegetables, spices and herbs.

biriyani: A dish of rice mixed with vegetables or meat or eggs, perfumed with spices like cardamom and saffron, and garnished with fried onions and fresh coriander. This is a popular dish for festivals, weddings, weekend meals, and special occasions.

chapati: A version of Indian bread, thinner than a naan, made of wheat or other grain flours. It is a staple on Indian dining tables. It is usually eaten with sabzi and dal, but kids (and many adults!) like to eat it with jam, or with ghee and sugar.

ghee: Clarified butter made by heating butter made from cream. When added to food, it imparts a rich taste and fragrance. Often used to make sweets, festive meals, or as a garnish on food for children.

vala: A bright green drink made with khus (edible vetiver grass) syrup and lots of sugar. Fizzy when made with soda but can be made with water too.

pachak: A digestive drink with a very strong taste, made with soda, ginger, lemon juice, pepper, rock salt, cumin and salt.

boondi: Tiny balls of deep-fried dough made from chickpea flour. Can be salted and eaten as a savoury, or soaked in sugar syrup and eaten as a sweet snack.

jalebi: Deep-fried sweets soaked in sugar syrup. Very popular in different forms across India.

dabga: A form of cooking used on occasion, not usually for daily meals. An earthen pot is stuffed with vegetables, sealed shut with straw, and buried under a bonfire. The heat from the fire steams the vegetables in their own juices, making them tender, moist, and smoke-flavoured.

gajar halwa: A soft type of dessert made by grating sweet winter carrots, mixing with sugar and milk and boiling until thick and sweet.

bekaar bachche: The literal translation is 'useless children' or 'good for nothing kids'.

kurta pyjama: A man's outfit made of thin material, with a long knee-length shirt, worn over loose trousers with a drawstring instead of elastic.

beta: The literal translation is 'son', also used as a term of endearment.

attar: A perfume oil made from natural floral or herbal ingredients, often used like an essential oil and mixed with carrier oils to use in personal care, as a perfume, or in the home.

naada: The drawstring used to hold up a skirt or pyjamas.

Rishte mein to hum tumhaare baap hote hain, naam hai Shahenshah: A popular line from 1988 Bollywood action movie Shahenshah, starring Amitabh Bachan.

Shahenshah: See above

pichkari: A squirt gun used by kids in water fights, especially during the festival of Holi.

naale ba: The literal translation (Kannada) is 'Come tomorrow'.

haldi: Turmeric, a spice or herb in powder or root form, said to have multiple healing powers.

nawab-sahib: Refers to nawabs or rulers/aristocrats in ancient India.

baba: Used here as a term of affection.

Keep up with new releases, subscribe to my bookish newsletter, and lots more at:

www.mishanakhot.com

www.mishanakhot.com

Printed in Great Britain
by Amazon